You're About to Become a

Privileged Woman.

INTRODUCING
PAGES & PRIVILEGES™.

It's our way of thanking you for buying
our books at your favorite retail store.

— *GET ALL THIS FREE* —
WITH JUST ONE PROOF OF PURCHASE:

◆ Hotel Discounts up to 60% at home and abroad

◆ Travel Service - Guaranteed lowest published
airfares plus 5% cash back on tickets

◆ $25 Travel Voucher

◆ Sensuous Petite Parfumerie collection ($50 value)

◆ Insider Tips Letter with ... s of
upcoming bo...

◆ Mystery G... before 6/15/95)

You'll get a FREE personal card, too.
It's your passport to all these benefits– and to
even more great gifts & benefits to come!

There's no club to join. No purchase commitment. No obligation.

As a Privileged Woman, you'll be entitled to all these *Free Benefits*. And *Free Gifts*, too.

To thank you for buying our books, we've designed an exclusive FREE program called *PAGES & PRIVILEGES*™. You can enroll with just one Proof of Purchase, and get the kind of luxuries that, until now, you could only read about.

*B*IG HOTEL DISCOUNTS

A privileged woman stays in the finest hotels. And so can you—at up to 60% off! Imagine standing in a hotel check-in line and watching as the guest in front of you pays $150 for the same room that's only costing you $60. Your *Pages & Privileges* discounts are good at Sheraton, Marriott, Best Western, Hyatt and thousands of other fine hotels all over the U.S., Canada and Europe.

*F*REE DISCOUNT TRAVEL SERVICE

A privileged woman is always jetting to romantic places.
When <u>you</u> fly, just make one phone call for the lowest published airfare at time of booking—<u>or double the difference back</u>! PLUS—

you'll get a $25 voucher to use the first time you book a flight AND <u>5% cash back on every ticket you buy thereafter through the travel service</u>!

FREE GIFTS!

A privileged woman is always getting wonderful gifts.
Luxuriate in rich fragrances that will stir your senses (and his). This gift-boxed assortment of fine perfumes includes three popular scents, each in a beautiful designer bottle. <u>Truly Lace</u>...This luxurious fragrance unveils your sensuous side. <u>L'Effleur</u>...discover the romance of the Victorian era with this soft floral. <u>Muguet des bois</u>...a single note floral of singular beauty. This $50 value is yours—FREE when you enroll in *Pages & Privileges*! And it's just the beginning of the gifts and benefits that will be coming your way!

FREE INSIDER TIPS LETTER

A privileged woman is always informed. And you'll be, too, with our free letter full of fascinating information and sneak previews of upcoming books.

MORE GREAT GIFTS & BENEFITS TO COME

A privileged woman always has a lot to look forward to.
And so will you. You get all these wonderful FREE gifts and benefits now with only one purchase...and there are no additional purchases required. However, each additional retail purchase of Harlequin and Silhouette books brings you a step closer to even more great FREE benefits like half-price movie tickets...and even more FREE gifts like these beautiful fragrance gift baskets:

L'Effleur...This basketful of romance lets you discover L'Effleur from head to toe, heart to home.

Truly Lace...A basket spun with the sensuous luxuries of Truly Lace, including Dusting Powder in a reusable satin and lace covered box.

ENROLL NOW!

Complete the Enrollment Form on the back of this card and become a Privileged Woman today!

**Enroll Today in *PAGES & PRIVILEGES*™,
the program that gives you Great Gifts
and Benefits with just one purchase!**

Enrollment Form

☐ *Yes!* I WANT TO BE A *P*RIVILEGED *W*OMAN.

Enclosed is one *PAGES & PRIVILEGES*™ Proof of Purchase from
any Harlequin or Silhouette book currently for sale in stores (Proofs of
Purchase are found on the back pages of books) and the store cash register
receipt. Please enroll me in *PAGES & PRIVILEGES*™. Send my Welcome
Kit and FREE Gifts -- and activate my FREE benefits -- immediately.

NAME (please print)

ADDRESS   APT. NO

CITY   STATE   ZIP/POSTAL CODE

PROOF OF PURCHASE

Please allow 6-8 weeks for delivery. Quantities are
limited. We reserve the right to substitute items.
Enroll before October 31, 1995 and receive
one full year of benefits.

**NO CLUB!
NO COMMITMENT!**
*Just one purchase brings
you great Free Gifts
and Benefits!*
(See inside for details.)

Name of store where this book was purchased_____

Date of purchase_____

Type of store:

☐ Bookstore   ☐ Supermarket   ☐ Drugstore

☐ Dept. or discount store (e.g. K-Mart or Walmart)

☐ Other (specify)_____

Which Harlequin or Silhouette series do you usually read?

_____

Complete and mail with one Proof of Purchase and store receipt to:

U.S.: *PAGES & PRIVILEGES*™, P.O. Box 1960, Danbury, CT 06813-1960

Canada: *PAGES & PRIVILEGES*™, 49-6A The Donway West, P.O. 813,
North York, ON M3C 2E8   PRINTED IN U.S.A

"What are we going to do?"

Reid's mouth set in a grim line. "The best defense is a good offense, and I intend to start offending right now."

"What do you have in mind?" Penny asked.

"The announcement of our engagement!"

Penny felt as if she'd been poleaxed. "What? You must be out of your mind! I'm not marrying you!"

Dear Reader,

When I was fifteen and overweight, (some things change, I'm no longer fifteen!), I wrote to a famous Australian woman, founder of a large-size fashion label. Her answer inspired me to follow my dreams regardless of size, shape or other limitations.

So when Harlequin suggested a letter as a springboard to romance, I immediately pictured a fan letter. There's a Suzie Kimber in all of us, with her youthful hopes and yearnings. And a Penny Sullivan, too, hearing the music of love and responding as we all dream of doing. May your dreams shine as brightly as hers.

Love,

Valerie Parv

P.S. I LOVE YOU
Valerie Parv

All rights reserved. Except for use in any review, the reproduction or utilization of this work in whole or in part in any form by any electronic, mechanical or other means, now known or hereafter invented, including xerography, photocopying and recording, or in any information storage or retrieval system, is forbidden without the permission of the publisher, Harlequin Enterprises Limited, 225 Duncan Mill Road, Don Mills, Ontario, Canada M3B 3K9.

Harlequin Books

TORONTO • NEW YORK • LONDON
AMSTERDAM • PARIS • SYDNEY • HAMBURG
STOCKHOLM • ATHENS • TOKYO • MILAN
MADRID • WARSAW • BUDAPEST • AUCKLAND

ISBN 0-373-03366-4

P.S. I LOVE YOU

CHAPTER ONE

Dear Mr Branden,

Hello. My name is Suzanne Kimber and I'm a big, big fan of yours. I'm sure you receive thousands of letters but this one is different so please, please read on.

I am fourteen and play the clarinet. My schoolhas a mentor programme where students invite someone from the music world to give them professional guidance. As I know no one in the music world, I decided to ask the greatest clarinettist there is to be my mentor.

I have studied the clarinet since primary school. I can't hope to emulate your feat of recording your first solo album at fourteen, but I would like to follow in your footsteps, playing and recording professionally, eventually becoming involved in music production. Like you, I might even have my own recording company one day.

Your time is valuable and I wouldn't intrude too much. A mentor mainly answers questions by mail and comments on tapes of the student's playing. Will you do this for me? Please?

Yours sincerely,

Suzanne (Suzie) Kimber

PS I especially love your playing of the Andretti Concerto. It gives me goose-bumps.

Reid Branden stared at the typewritten sheet of paper which vibrated ever so slightly in his long-fingered hand. His steely gaze was fixed on the last line, added in a schoolgirlish scrawl completely at odds with the shock the words punched through him. How the devil had a child he'd never met managed to hear the Andretti?

'What is it, another crank? I thought I filtered most of them out.'

He favoured his assistant, Tonia Rigg, with a wintry smile. 'It isn't a crank. You do a perfect job of screening them and you know it. It's this request for me to be a musical mentor to a schoolgirl.' He rolled his eyes. 'When will they stop regarding me as some kind of pop star?'

'When you stop looking like one,' Tonia rejoined.

Impatiently he pushed back the thatch of toast-brown hair which he was blissfully unaware contributed to his image problem. 'How can I look like a pop star? I don't even perform live any more. What's sexy about a thirty-year-old corporate executive and music administrator?' His palm slid across his rock-hard stomach. 'Hell, I may even be developing a paunch.'

'And I'm the Hunchback of Notre Dame,' she threw back. 'Apart from your film-star looks, it's the recordings that do it. Who else do you know who can put Mozart in the Top Ten?'

'Then maybe it's time I stopped recording and concentrated on the business.'

She affected a shudder. 'Concentrate any harder on the business and we'll have to move to a tax haven.'

He welcomed the diversion. 'Speaking of moving, how have you recovered from the switch from Los Angeles to North Sydney?'

'I miss the excitement and pace of LA,' she admitted, 'but Australia has its charms, not the least of which is that gorgeous penthouse you organised for me. How's your own home-hunt going?'

'Slowly. I'm sick to death of living in the executive quarters upstairs. I'm looking around for a house.'

Her finely pencilled eyebrows lifted. 'So the move back here is permanent?'

'I told you it was. Now the American arm is running smoothly, I can focus on the Australian operation. It's been my goal all along.'

'I know. You were always a true-blue Aussie at heart.' She reached for the letter which rested in his fingers. 'Shall I handle this? Send the usual form letter and signed photograph?'

'No.' His tone sharpened unintentionally and he forced a smile. 'I'll take care of this one myself.' As soon as he found out where she'd heard the Andretti, he added inwardly.

Tonia looked put out. 'In that case, would you like to take care of this pile as well?' She gestured towards the overflowing in-tray. 'There's a couple of marriage proposals which may interest you.'

He shook his head, his gaze softening. 'No, thanks. You're doing a great job and I don't wish to interfere. But this one intrigues me. I'd like to look into it before deciding what to do.' At least until he found out what was going on.

Her graceful smile acknowledged his right to do crazy things if he chose. 'You're the boss. I'll get on to it as soon as you dictate a reply.'

'Have I told you how valuable you are to me?'

'Not often enough.'

'Then consider yourself told. I dread the day you announce you're giving all this up to get married.'

Her tart look surprised him. 'How old-fashioned can you get? People don't give up their work just because they get married any more. Assuming I had any such notions, of course.'

'Don't you?'

Bleakness invaded her expression. 'Oh, I have them, all right. But you know the saying, it takes two to tango.'

'I know.' Her wishes couldn't be plainer if she'd stated them outright, which she had on the odd occasion they'd shared a bottle of wine late into the evening. He'd even tried to feel as she did but nothing came. Knowing it was his fault that she was still unattached added to the punchy feeling the letter had aroused in him. 'Why don't you take the rest of the day off? You must have a lot to do at home.'

She picked up the basket of correspondence. 'Maybe I will.' But he knew she wouldn't. Tonia Rigg was as devoted to him as any wife. It was a damned shame that, try as he might, he couldn't see her in the role.

As the door closed behind her he turned back to the letter he still clutched in tense fingers. He made an effort to relax his hand and the page drifted to the desk top where it lay in mute accusation.

Accusation of what?

Penny Sullivan, that was what. In his mind she and the Andretti Concerto were inseparable.

He wished he could say he hadn't thought of her in five years but he had, often. Her natural charm and unaffected beauty haunted him, although he hadn't seen her in that time.

Did she still wear her hair in a soft curtain around her face, a wisp above collar-length so it swished when she moved? He recalled it was an unusual colour—sunny bronze, he described it. She thought herself too curvy to be beautiful but the combination of a tiny waist and full hips put all sorts of thoughts in his head, none of them to do with business.

Her eyes were startling, too. Wide apart, a warm amber colour and always sparkling. Or they had been until their last meeting.

It had taken place only a few days after they returned to Sydney from Canberra where he'd given a successful charity concert. At least successful as far as the charity was concerned. For Penny it had been another story. 'You're behaving like a child,' he'd told her curtly. 'Anyone can make a mistake. What's so terrible about admitting it and going on from there?'

Her hands had lifted as if she were trying to fend off a blow. 'That's the problem. You believe I made the mistake, don't you?'

'You can't deny that you were behind the wheel when my car ploughed into that wall. You were the one who wanted to leave early. I gave you the car

keys myself on condition you used one of the
courtesy drivers, which you didn't see fit to do, despite the fact that you'd been drinking.'

'It was a cocktail party to celebrate the concert.
Of course I had,' she repeated in the weary tone of
one who has told the same tale more times than she
liked to think. 'I remember you giving me the keys
but I don't remember getting into the car. It's all
a blank from the time you told me you'd join us
at the hotel later, until you were looming over me
at the scene of the accident.'

'You were lucky I decided to follow almost immediately. If anyone had been hurt and the police
had been called . . .'

'I know, I'd have been charged with driving under
the influence of alcohol, so I have you to thank for
saving my neck.' And his own reputation, she
couldn't help thinking. Even while Reid's doctor
had been checking her and Tonia over, Tonia could
only ramble on about how important it was that
nothing of the accident should be made public in
case it reflected badly on Reid. They were part of
his public family, Tonia was fond of reminding
Penny archly.

Nothing had got out, and the bump on Penny's
head which had left her unable to recall much of
anything between the party and waking up after the
accident had developed into no more than a mild
concussion. It was a minor miracle because the car
had been a write-off. Reid hadn't cared about the
car. It was replaceable. Tonia and Penny were not.

His forbearance hadn't been enough for Penny. 'I can't stand having you think I'd *do* such a thing,' she told him. 'Especially knowing how you feel about people who drink and drive.'

'Is it any wonder, considering one of them killed my parents?'

'There, you see? The tone you use, the way you look when you remember how they were taken from you when you were only fifteen—I'm terrified that the day will come when you'll look at me like that.'

'That has nothing to do with you and me.'

Her delicate features had begun to crumble but she shrank back when he moved to comfort her. 'Don't, please. I don't want your...your forgiveness.' She said it as if it was a mortal insult. 'I want you to give me the benefit of the doubt.'

His patience had finally snapped. 'What doubt? You were behind the wheel, for pity's sake.'

Her eyes had gleamed wetly but she held her head high. 'Therefore I must have been driving, right? No other explanation is possible.'

'None which makes any sense.'

He had blamed her persistence on the shock of the accident. What else could he do? Hadn't he pulled her out of the driver's seat with his own hands? His blood still ran cold when he thought of how easily it could have been her lifeless body. Because of a mistake she wasn't willing to admit to, he could have lost both her and Tonia that night.

As it turned out, he had lost Penny anyway. Soon after the accident she left her copywriting job at the advertising agency where he'd met her and went to England to work. Although she plainly didn't want to be found he could have used his network of contacts to track her down, but what was the point?

It was over between them. The only legacy of those torrid months was a piece of music written at white-heat to celebrate their affair—the Andretti Concerto, named, rather foolishly he thought now, for their favourite Italian restaurant. He had dedicated it to Penny. Its first—hell, it's only— playing had been preserved on a rough demo cassette he'd intended to polish later for performance. On the night of the accident, he'd given it to Penny to play. Afterwards, they'd had more pressing things to worry about.

He never did find out what she thought of the music, or if she'd even played it at all. He neither knew nor cared. It was one piece of music he never wanted to play again.

He had certainly never recorded it. So how could this—he consulted the letter—Suzanne Kimber claim to have heard it? He did some fast arithmetic. Penny would be twenty-six now, too young to have a fourteen-year-old daughter, assuming he'd been so careless. He was caught off guard by a hollow sensation which accompanied the thought, but thrust it away. So who was she?

The notepaper with its school crest offered no clues. The name Kimber meant nothing to him. Yet somehow, somewhere, she'd come across a piece of music meant for one woman in the world. He knew he wouldn't rest until he found the connection.

Inspiration made him thumb the intercom. 'Yes, boss?' came Tonia's instant response from the office beyond his own.

'Are you still here?' He affected a gruff tone.

'You gave me the afternoon off. It's two minutes to noon,' she retorted crisply. 'Shall I put them to good use or waste them defending myself to you?'

'Smart witch. Just as well you're invaluable,' he growled. 'Here's your chance to prove it. Was there by any chance a return envelope with the letter from the Kimber girl?'

He heard papers rustling. 'Yes, there was. I kept it aside thinking I'd be answering it.'

His chest felt tight suddenly and he thanked years of musical training for the control he was able to exert over his breathing. 'I suppose the address is some college she goes to?'

'As a matter of fact it isn't. The foolish child can't have been warned about stranger danger because the envelope's hand-written and addressed to her at a place called Kangaluma at Neutral Bay. Pretty fancy location.'

Not if it was the house he remembered, he thought grimly as memory came crashing back. He had his connection, although he still didn't know what it meant, but he was going to find out.

'Shall I bring in the envelope?'

'No, thanks, Tonia. You've given me all the answer I need for the moment.' Thank goodness for the teenager's naïveté, he thought as he switched off the intercom. She had obviously been meant to use her school address but had slipped up when it came to the return envelope. Now all he had to do was follow the trail and see where it led him.

CHAPTER TWO

'THAT'S the third time you've checked the letterbox since you got home from school,' Penny chided gently. 'What are you hoping for, a lottery win?'

Her niece's golden features coloured rosily. 'I was hoping to hear from Reid Branden by now. It's been two whole weeks.'

'Two weeks isn't long to a man in his position,' Penny consoled automatically, hardly looking up from her computer screen where a sales letter for an insurance company was taking shape. Suddenly her fingers froze on the keys. Oh, no, Suzie wouldn't have? 'Didn't you type the letter on school stationery? Wouldn't he send his reply to the school?'

Suzie squirmed uncomfortably. 'I did put it on school letterhead but...'

'But what?' Penny could hardly speak for the lump filling her throat. She hadn't wanted to be involved in the project at all and had only helped Suzie to draft the letter because it meant so much to her. Her niece had no conception of the toll it took on Penny herself. Even after five years there was still a raw place in her heart when she thought of Reid Branden, and what could have been.

The letter had Suzie's signature but that didn't help. There was still the agony of picturing him handling the sheet of paper, reading the words

Penny had written. She cursed her writer's imagination which made the images so cruelly vivid.

'Suzie?' she prompted hoarsely when the silence dragged on.

'The teacher said we should use our initiative so I did,' she said, her tone defiant. 'I added a PS in my own handwriting and put in a return envelope with this address on it. I thought his answer would get here quicker that way.'

Anguish speared through Penny. 'Suzie, you didn't?'

'Well, I'll be here for another month till Mum and Dad get back from overseas. I couldn't very well use our address, could I?'

'But now he knows where you live.' Where I live, a heartsick inner voice added.

Suzie misunderstood the reason for Penny's distress. 'It's not as if he's a weirdo or anything. He's famous and respectable, so it was all right to use this address, wasn't it?' Something in Penny's stricken expression made her drop her voice uncertainly.

'What did you write in the postscript?'

Suzie looked embarrassed. 'I told him how listening to his recordings gave me goose-bumps. I don't even know why I added it. Maybe you'd done such a great job on the letter that I wanted to add something of my own. Do you think I blew it?'

Her tragic expression stirred Penny's compassion. 'Of course you didn't blow it. Advertising psychologists say that the PS is the best-read part of any sales letter. Your instincts were spot-on.'

Suzie's moist eyes brightened. 'Really? Everything's cool, then. I know I should have asked you about it but I'm glad you're not mad at me.'

'I'm not mad at you,' Penny agreed on a heavy sigh. The child didn't know about her previous involvement with Reid Branden when she was a copywriter working with the agency which handled his recording company. Suzie's family had been living half a continent away in Adelaide at the time.

Not for a nine-year-old the anguish of falling in love with someone so far outside her orbit that it had seemed like a miracle. To Penny, Reid Branden had been the man of her dreams. She could hardly believe he was interested in the unsophisticated twenty-one-year-old she'd been then.

The only complication had been his beautiful personal assistant, Tonia Rigg. Penny could still remember Tonia's frosty comment when Penny arrived at their office to discuss headlines for a forthcoming advertisement she had been delegated to write.

'What are you here for, work experience?'

To her annoyance, Penny had flushed scarlet as she stammered out her identity and purpose. The woman had managed to make her feel young and gauche.

She was acutely conscious that her chainstore clothes were no match for Tonia's designer-label gear. Tonia's family was wealthy, someone at the agency told Penny. She didn't really need to work as Reid's assistant, although it was plain why she did so.

Had Tonia succeeded in marrying her boss by now? There hadn't been any headlines but Reid might have used his influence to keep the union private.

At the thought of Reid marrying Tonia, pure white-hot pain lanced through Penny. She was unaware of voicing a protest until Suzie put a hand on her shoulder. 'Are you OK?'

She forced a shaky smile. 'I'm fine. I've been sitting too long at this keyboard. It's giving me a cramp.'

'You know what you tell me. Go out and stretch your muscles, get some fresh air.'

In spite of her inner turmoil, Penny laughed. 'You sound just like your mother.' At eight years her senior, Jo was fond of giving Penny advice. Suzie had exactly captured Jo's sister-knows-best tone.

Suzie frowned. 'Is that good or bad?'

Penny ruffled her niece's silky blonde hair. 'Neither. It's what your mother would call a statement of fact.' She filed the sales letter on to a disk and stood up. 'But you're right, I could use some fresh air. The deadline for this isn't until tomorrow. You can use the computer for your homework if you like.'

At the mention of the dreaded word, Suzie's face fell. 'I was going to come outside with you.'

Penny pushed her firmly into her newly vacated chair. Much as she enjoyed Suzie's company, she felt a strong need to be alone with her thoughts for a while. 'Homework first, young lady.'

'Now who sounds like my mother?'

The grumbling continued under her breath but Penny was reassured by the tapping of keys, which receded as she let herself out of the house.

The steep path which ended at the harbour's edge needed weeding again, she noticed guiltily. She'd been too busy earning a living and looking after Suzie to do much work around the garden lately, although work there was in plenty.

How wonderful it must have been when the house was built in the late 1800s to have an army of gardeners to maintain the acres which had surrounded the house originally. With time the land had dwindled to a few hundred square metres but they still needed regular attention.

Maybe Jo was right in urging her to sell. The proceeds would give her the means to buy a modest flat and some capital to invest for security. Jo had even offered to give Penny her share of the house, since her own marriage ensured she was comfortably provided for.

Penny had turned this suggestion down flat. When their father died he had left the property to them jointly, with the provision that Penny be allowed to live in the house for as long as she needed to.

It was a generous enough arrangement. Penny couldn't take further advantage of Jo's generosity. She was determined to buy her sister out, although saving the money was proving much harder than she had imagined, given the expense of maintaining the house at the same time.

There was only one other way she would consider leaving Kangaluma—and that was if she fell

madly in love and wanted to marry. The prospect
seemed an impossible fantasy. After Reid, her re-
lationships had been few in number and superficial
in nature. How could she trust herself to love again,
knowing how easily it could end in heartache?

Loving hurt and leaving hurt worse, she told
herself. Devoting herself to the upkeep of
Kangaluma was far less painful. If it left her feeling
empty and alone sometimes, it was the price she
had decided to pay.

She didn't expect Jo to share her attachment to
the old house. Jo hadn't lived here since her marriage to Andrew Kimber but Penny's only absence
had been the two years spent working in London
until her father's illness brought her home to care
for him. Home to generations of Sullivans almost
from the convict era, the house was his legacy, one
Penny felt passionate about holding on to.

Not that there was a lot to hold on to right now,
she thought wistfully, turning to face the house. So
much work needed doing to put the house to rights
that money was a constant worry. Her father had
spent money as fast as he earned it, leaving almost
nothing towards Kangaluma's upkeep.
Nevertheless, from where she stood, it was a romantic sight with its old-world Elizabethan gables,
ficus and ivy-covered walls, turreted chimney-pots
and roof of old blue and red tiles weathered to a
hundred mellow tints.

From this side, one entered the house from a
broad veranda, arriving at a spacious oak-roofed
hall. Upstairs was a warren of quaint little rooms

reached by a winding stairway which terminated in a miniature tower.

It was the dining-room on the ground floor, with its mullioned windows, arched roof and old manorial fireplace, which Penny loved the best. In here, taking up the whole of one wall, were the faded remains of a striking mural depicting the arrival of the First Fleet ship, *Sirius*, into Sydney Cove. It was one of only two such frescoes in Australia, painted by a famous artist who was at one time, marine painter to the Queen. Legend had it that he painted the mural in return for hospitality from one of Penny's forebears.

Reid had been impressed by the fresco, Penny recalled with a pang. He had stood beside her on this very spot, mapping out the restoration of Kangaluma, which he agreed was vital. He would never have agreed with the idea of selling.

As if his opinion mattered now, Penny thought, turning towards the harbour so the sea breeze tugged at her hair. She was probably worrying needlessly that he would connect her with Suzie's letter just because of a return address on an envelope. Given the heights he had scaled in the music world since they parted, he probably didn't even remember her name.

Why couldn't she be equally blasé about him, she asked herself despairingly. Five years should be enough to dim the memory of their relationship. It probably would have been if she weren't continually confronted by his image in the media, she assured herself.

Who did she think she was fooling?

Even if she had never seen his likeness since they parted, it would be burned on her memory as if with a brand.

From the moment he had asked her out—to discuss business, as she had naïvely assumed—awareness had flamed between them, almost incandescent in its intensity. He had pushed aside the notepad and pen she had brought with her and taken her hands across the table. 'I thought you wanted to discuss copy for the concert programme,' she had stammered.

His smouldering eyes had burned into her. 'Do *you* want to discuss the copy?'

Her voice had almost deserted her. 'No.'

'Good. Then we can talk about much more important matters such as the remarkable colour of your eyes and whether you do anything to your hair to make it curl across your forehead so enticingly.' He had wound a strand around his finger to illustrate.

Very little business had been transacted that evening, or on any of the other occasions they spent together. He provided her with tickets to his friends' concerts and broadened her musical education with whispered commentaries as he held her hand in the dark.

It wasn't the only area of her education he broadened, she thought, reddening at the memory. He was so much more worldly than she was and had taken her to heights of sensation she had never dreamed men and women could achieve. He had been the most tender, considerate yet exciting of lovers, making her feel like a rare and precious jewel he valued beyond price.

If only he had accompanied her and Tonia when they'd left that after-concert party in Canberra five years ago. But the media had wanted more interviews and Tonia had been impatient to return to their hotel. 'When you've been to one of these affairs, you've been to them all. Let's go.'

She had several drinks, too, and it was making her even more difficult than usual, Penny recalled. She would have waited for Reid but was worried about the other woman and had agreed to accompany her back to the hotel. She would give anything to have that decision to make over again.

She dimly recalled a valet bringing Reid's car around for them but everything afterwards was a frightening blur. A rainy night. Streets slippery as glass with a confusion of reflected street-lights, traffic lights and signs were jumbled together in her memory. In her dreams she heard shrieks of terror blended with the sickening crunch of the car slamming into something, followed by eerie silence. Awake, she couldn't piece together even that much.

She had woken up confused and disorientated, to find Reid lifting her out of the mangled car and placing her into another car, borrowed from a friend she discovered later. She and Tonia were whisked to the hotel and placed in the care of Reid's personal physician. The verdict was cuts and bruises, and a possible concussion on Penny's part. Nothing which rest and care wouldn't mend.

All except her memory of exactly what happened. She vaguely remembered arguing with Tonia over who should drive, but nothing afterwards. *Was* Reid right? Had she insisted on driving despite having drunk several cocktails at the reception?

According to Tonia she had, and there was no doubt that she was behind the wheel when Reid found them. Beyond that, she had only her own belief that she had tried to stop Tonia from driving, but not by taking the wheel herself. Without proof, she wasn't even sure in her own mind who was in the right.

The censure in Reid's voice when they'd discussed it had cut her to the quick. No matter how he'd tried to conceal it, he was plainly disappointed in her. How long would it have been before he began to hold that night against her, perhaps when they had their first serious disagreement?

She had seen it all before in her parents' marriage, after her father had succumbed to temptation and had an affair with a colleague at the school where he taught art and history. Penny's mother had been devastated but had finally forgiven him and the marriage had continued. But she had used the lapse against him in every subsequent altercation until she had died of pneumonia when Penny was thirteen.

She and Jo weren't supposed to know anything about their father's affair, but it had been hard to remain in ignorance when the subject was raised in so many subtle ways during their childhood.

Remembering her father's anguish every time his lapse was brought up had convinced Penny that she couldn't bear to be in the same situation. Rather than take the risk, she had severed her tie with Reid, although it had almost killed her at the time. But when she married she wanted it to be with a clean slate and no past transgressions which could be used against her.

Lost in thought, she followed the path to a gazebo the family called Jack's Folly after her father's insistence on building it—not after his affair, she thought wryly. Her mother had referred to it by that name rather more often than Penny thought necessary, another reminder of his fall from grace.

The structure was ramshackle now, half hidden by the Edna Walling roses trailing over it. Near the entrance a Victorian urn lay on its side, succulents blossoming from every crack, mingling with the geraniums and nicotiana which had escaped from once-neat garden beds.

She sighed. So much needed doing but she was hard-pressed to keep the place going at all, especially on the erratic income of a freelance copywriter. Even so, she made more than she would working for someone else. But the property soaked up money like a sponge.

Face it, the house isn't on your mind at the moment, she told herself sternly. You're trying to avoid thinking about what will happen if Reid answers Suzie's letter. Could she deal with seeing him again?

He was more likely to send a form letter and a polite refusal. These days he was too much the high-flyer to have time to sponsor a schoolgirl musician. He now headed a substantial recording empire which specialised in bringing classical music into popular play. It had always been his dream.

She stiffened as an involuntary image of his fingers moving up and down his clarinet sprang into her mind. No, she wouldn't think of him now. Why on earth hadn't she persuaded Suzie to choose some other person in the music world as her mentor?

'Hello, Penny.'

Startled, she spun around, her eyes flaring as she caught sight of the commanding figure framed in the entrance to the gazebo. Had she conjured him out of her own turbulent thoughts? 'No,' she said on a hissing note of consternation. He couldn't be here. She wasn't ready.

Anger flickered across his handsome features before he schooled them into impassivity. 'No?' His eyebrow tilted ironically. 'A refusal so quickly, Penny? I haven't asked you anything yet.'

She recoiled from the amusement in his voice. He might find this diverting, but she was far from amused by his sudden appearance in her sanctuary. '"No" seems a good word for anything you might want to ask me,' she said, annoyed by the betraying tremor she heard in her voice. Her limbs felt icy and she linked her hands together in an unconsciously defensive gesture. 'It was a word we used quite often when last we met.'

'A word you used,' he corrected coldly. 'It looks as if nothing has changed.'

A shiver gripped her as the years abruptly fell away and she saw him as she'd last seen him, coming to take her to a concert at the Opera House.

She'd chosen to wait in the summerhouse to have a few moments alone with him before they set off.

He'd looked much as he did now—breathtakingly handsome, carrying his broadly masculine frame with a confidence bordering on arrogance. Then, as now, she had caught her breath at the sheer male magnetism he exuded.

His kiss had been feverish, returned with equal fervour by her as she'd felt the warmth of his hands splaying across her bared shoulders. Tentatively she had asked whether they would be missed at the concert.

His teasing look had made her want to melt. 'Is this the same shy little copywriter I used to know?'

Never shy with him, she had thought, marvelling as his caressing tone filled her with joy. On his arm she'd felt like a queen.

Then the vision changed and she saw again the raw, vulnerable woman he had pulled from the wreckage. Remembered guilt, pain and humiliation flared through her as she remembered the condemnation on his face even as he said the words of forgiveness.

He would forgive but he wouldn't forget, she had thought. And he hadn't forgotten, she realised as she witnessed the interplay of emotions on his face. Was he remembering how he had recoiled in disgust from the liquor tainting her breath, telling its tale of reckless irresponsibility? How could he not think of it now as he looked at her?

She turned away, facing the harbour through the tangle of greenery, forcing her breathing to slow. If only his very presence didn't remind her of her culpability. The shock of her brush with death lived with her to this day, making her an exemplary driver. She never wanted anyone to look at her with the horror she had seen on Reid's face that night.

It was over in an instant but the recollections—one so sweet it made her want to cry, the other cruelly painful—stayed with her as she fought for control. 'If nothing's changed, why are you here?' she managed to ask, her tone vibrant.

'You invited me to come.'

Her hunted gaze travelled around the gazebo but the only way out was past him. 'I invited you? You must be mistaken.'

'Do you deny writing to me about participating in a mentor programme?'

'My niece, Suzanne Kimber, wrote to you. She's the one who contacted you, not me.'

'That's garbage and you know it.' He met her startled look unwaveringly. 'Regardless of who signed the letter, you wrote it, didn't you?'

What difference did it make? 'Very well, I drafted it for Suzie. How did you know?'

'You forget we worked together for some time. I recognise your style. Besides, you had to be behind her mention of the Andretti Concerto.'

Her fingers flew to her mouth. 'But I didn't...'

'No, but Suzie did. She added a PS in which she stated that my playing of the Andretti gave her goose-bumps. You and I both know there's only one place she could possibly have heard that piece of music, one person who could have played it for her.'

Her mouth went dry. 'Once. She heard me play it once and asked me what it was. I thought she'd forgotten all about it.'

'Evidently not. It seems to have made a greater impact on her than on the woman it was written for.'

If only it were true. Her mind reeled as she recalled how many times she had played the tape to console herself at some dark moment. The sweetly haunting melody, recorded without any artifice, just as Reid had written it, had the power to move her beyond the greatest symphonies ever composed because it was *her* music.

Suzie had heard it on such an occasion, the first anniversary of Penny's father's death. Normally she would have made sure she was alone, but this time the anniversary had dulled her sense of caution. She had played the tape in her room, forgetting that Suzie was due to visit. Penny hadn't even registered the teenager's presence in her doorway until her rapturous sigh followed the last lingering notes of clarinet music.

Before Penny could stop her, Suzie had waltzed to the tape deck and fished out the cassette, reading the title in Reid's own hand on one side. Of course she hadn't recognised the writing but nothing could disguise the unique playing style.

'I thought it was Reid Branden,' she commented with satisfaction. 'I don't recognise this piece, though. What is it?'

'It's called the Andretti Concerto. One of my clients is thinking of using it as backing for a new

TV commercial,' she had improvised, trusting this would explain the raw quality of the recording.

'They should. It's awesome.' Suzie accepted the explanation. 'If they use it, will you get to work with him?'

'Probably not. They would buy the rights and get a session musician to record it. Branden would never do a commercial.'

Suzie's face had fallen but she had allowed the subject to be changed, to Penny's intense relief. Sharing the music even with someone who appreciated it as much as Suzie did was too much like baring her soul.

She might have known that Suzie would remember the piece, but she had never dreamed she would mention it in her letter to Reid Branden. She might as well have shouted her relationship with Penny from the rooftops. He must have made the connection immediately.

And now he was here.

'I'm sure you didn't come to rake up dead embers,' she said, her heart constricting as if in a vice as she saw him wince at her choice of words. He couldn't know that it was an instinctively defensive gesture. More than anything she needed to put some emotional distance between them.

She had always assumed that if she saw him again things would be different. It had never occurred to her that the pull of his presence would be as powerful as ever, that the mere sight of him would awaken yearnings she'd believed long buried. Knowing the contempt in which he now held her, it was almost more than she could handle.

'Sometimes there's a spark even in apparently dead embers,' he observed. 'Often it only requires a breath to fan them into life.'

He took a step closer, his firm tread making the weathered floorboards creak. She shrank back against the latticed wall of the gazebo, fascinated against her will by the sight of his rugged features looming nearer and nearer.

Her brain dealt with the details in a flash. Hair slightly more receding than she remembered, emphasising his high, intelligent forehead. Coal-black brows drawn close together over the most unforgettable eyes in the world. They seemed to flare as they raked her, with that uncanny ability to change from hazel to green-blue. She held her breath as he reached her.

Her stomach churned. She didn't want him to touch her and yet...

With an oath he spun aside, but not before she saw his expression change. Her heart sank. There was no mistaking the distaste on his features and it could only be for her.

Anger hit her like a solid wall. Why hadn't she taken the initiative, pushing him aside and making it clear that there were no embers whatsoever to fan? Instead she had waited passively, hunger for his touch so obvious that he must have seen it, responding only until he remembered what she was capable of doing. He had forgiven but he hadn't forgotten. The truth was in his eyes before he looked away.

Rage boiled through her. 'Why don't you say it? Do I still drink and drive? I can see it's on your mind.'

His face was impassive when he turned back. 'It's obviously on yours so it doesn't matter what I say, does it?'

He didn't deny it, she noticed, tension clawing at her. She couldn't believe how chaotic her emotions had become in the few minutes since his appearance. It had to be because he reminded her of a night she would give anything to erase from her life, not because she still felt anything for him. She refused to believe otherwise. 'I think you'd better leave,' she said with as much dignity as she could muster.

'Still using retreat to solve your problems, Penny?'

'Retreat? I don't——'

'You don't know what I'm talking about,' he supplied, his harsh tone cutting her off. 'You didn't run away before, when the going got tough, and you aren't on the verge of doing it now. Like hell you aren't.'

Her chin came up. She might deserve his censure when it came to that fateful night, but she was not going to let him accuse her of cowardice. Leaving him had been the greatest act of courage in her life.

'You don't know anything about me any more,' she seethed. 'If I had planned to run away from my problems, I'd have sold this house instead of hanging on to it by the skin of my teeth. I wouldn't have come home to nurse my father through two years of watching heart disease kill him before my eyes. And I wouldn't be here talking to you now.'

A strange light flickered in the blue-green gaze. 'You've been through more than I realised. Perhaps your lack of courage is only where I'm concerned, although I question your need for courage on my account. Not so many years ago, all you needed was love.'

That was then, this is now, the bitter fact returned. Running a marathon could not have exhausted her more than this confrontation. 'I'm sorry you've wasted your time,' she forced herself to say formally. 'I'll tell Suzie this whole idea was a mistake.'

His eyes flamed. 'It may be to you, but not to me. I've no intention of disappointing your niece to salve your pride. So you can come back to the house with me voluntarily, or I can carry you there. Which is it to be?'

CHAPTER THREE

THE thought of being carried back to the house in Reid's arms was enough to lend wings to Penny's feet. She had no doubt that he meant it. Once before she had defied him in fun and he had lifted her effortlessly into arms of steel, ignoring all her pleas to set her down.

That scene had ended in laughter and kisses. Now it was more likely to end in tears and humiliation. She hurried ahead of him, all too aware of his long strides on the path beside her. His breath feathered the side of her neck, disturbing her hair and creating a hollow sensation all the way to her core.

Why did he have to come back now? What did he want from her? She had the feeling it was more than a wish to help a budding musician. Was it revenge because she had challenged his right to possess her? Surely wanting his trust rather than his forgiveness wasn't asking so much? Apparently he thought it was, because he had never come after her, never challenged Tonia's version of what happened. It was as if their relationship had crashed into the same brick wall as the car.

Suzie was still working at the computer when Penny showed Reid into the house. In spite of her own misgivings, the thought of Suzie's pleasure when she saw Reid gave her strength.

'You have a visitor, Suzie,' she said softly.

Without turning her head, Suzie grumbled, 'If it's Amanda, tell her I'm busy.'

Reid's eyes glinted wickedly. 'But it isn't Amanda.'

At the masculine voice, Suzie's head came up. Her stunned expression was worth all the pain Penny had endured in seeing Reid again. 'Holy hollyhocks, it *is* you, Reid, I mean Mr Branden.' Her hands went to her hair in the age-old preening gesture and her cheeks glowed bright red.

'Reid will be fine,' he assured her gravely. 'You must be Suzanne Kimber who wrote to me so eloquently.'

'Call me Suzie, please.' Her flustered gaze shot to Penny. 'I had some help with the letter,' she confessed. 'My Aunt Penny is a professional writer and she knew how much I wanted you as my mentor, so I hope you don't think it's cheating or anything.'

'No, it wasn't cheating. Getting help with a letter comes under the heading of enterprise, by my reckoning.'

'Thanks.' She jumped up. 'I should offer you a seat. Would you like some coffee? Penny made carrot cake this afternoon. I can get you some.'

He steered the flustered teenager to a chair and sat her down, dropping easily into its twin opposite. 'Why don't we let your aunt get the coffee while you tell me about your musical ambitions?'

His dismissal rankled slightly even as Penny recognised his strategy to put Suzie at ease. In the kitchen as she made the coffee, her mind seethed. Seeing his easy mastery of the situation reminded

her painfully of her own first meeting with him.
Like Suzie, she had been putty in his hands.

Through the half-open door she could see her
niece leaning towards him, her body language
telegraphing her adulation. Had Penny herself been
so pathetically eager to win his approval? Yes, she
had, she acknowledged reluctantly. And he had also
made her feel as if she was the only person who
mattered to him at that moment.

As she carried the tray through to the living-room
she almost collided with Suzie as she rocketed past.
'Reid wants me to play for him,' she said
breathlessly.

Moments later she was back carrying her
treasured Yamaha clarinet. Penny saw the approval
on Reid's face as Suzie carefully assembled and
aligned the instrument. There was a moment of
silence as Suzie steadied her breathing then she
launched into the Humoresque in B major, a piece
she had played for her last examination.

It was breathtakingly beautiful and even Penny
recognised the breadth of Suzie's talent. She was
suddenly glad that she had written the letter, even
if it meant steeling herself to see Reid again at
school recitals. Suzie deserved whatever help he
could give her.

When the young musician finished, Reid accorded her the rare respect of a long silence before
he put his palms gently together. 'Bravo, Suzie. You
play with the same kind of fire that I had at your
age.'

If possible, Suzie's colour deepened. 'Oh, no, I
can't compare myself to a virtuoso like you.'

'And neither should you. You must aim to develop your own style, a way of playing which is as unique as a signature, so that an audience can recognise your playing blindfolded.'

He went on to suggest some adjustments in Suzie's articulation. 'The flow of air should be constant, as if you're playing one long note,' he pointed out, taking the instrument from her to demonstrate.

Suzie experimented with a few notes and they were noticeably more mellow. If he could make such a difference in a few minutes, what might a longer association do for Suzie? Penny couldn't help thinking.

'We'll talk more when I come again,' he concluded, drawing an involuntary gasp of protest from Penny.

'No, you mustn't. I mean, this is a school project. They won't expect you to give up so much of your time, only to listen to her tapes and comment on them when you have the time.'

His level gaze held hers in thrall. 'You must recall that I don't do things by halves, Penny. If I'm going to help Suzie with her music, it won't be at arm's length.'

But it has to be, Penny's inner voice cried out. Otherwise it would be more than she could tolerate, couldn't he see that? 'Suzie, didn't you have to wash your hair today?' she reminded her niece pointedly. She wasn't about to continue this discussion in front of the teenager.

Suzie gave her a 'how could you' look but grudgingly dismantled her clarinet and stowed it into its case. 'Do you mean it about coming again?' she asked Reid.

His answering gaze encompassed Penny. 'I never say anything I don't mean.'

'Wow, this has been the greatest day of my life. Thank you...Reid.'

Her happiness cast a glow around the room, although Penny hardly shared the teenager's enthusiasm. All the same she was pleased to hear Suzie whistling under her breath as she half danced down the corridor to her room.

'She has a formidable talent,' Reid observed when they were alone.

'She's also young and vulnerable. I hope you'll keep it in mind,' Penny said more sharply than she intended.

'Are you referring to yourself or Suzie?' he asked mildly. When she didn't answer he picked up his coffee cup. 'Why is she staying with you? Trouble at home?'

'No. My sister, Jo, and her husband are touring South-east Asia and didn't want her to miss any schooling. I have plenty of room here, so...'

'Normally you live alone here?'

'Apart from my succession of live-in lovers, yes,' she retorted. The last thing she wanted was for him to feel sorry for her, or to conclude that because he was no longer in her life, she was living a nun's existence. It was close to being true but she had no intentions of telling him so.

He took in the computer atop the heavy oak desk and the bulky metal filing cabinet standing beside it. 'You work from home these days?'

'I've been freelancing since I returned from London to look after Dad. He died two years ago and I found I wanted to keep working for myself.' No need to tell him that agency jobs were at a premium now. Once she'd realised that for every job going in advertising there were at least fifty applicants, it had seemed more sensible to start her own business. As well, working from home had allowed her to earn an income while caring for her ailing father. Gradually it had become her way of life. She wasn't sure she would change it now if she could.

He leaned back in the chair, very much at ease although she felt as if she could explode at any moment. He had seen Suzie and heard her play. What more did he want?

'I didn't come here only to meet Suzie,' he stated when her nerves were stretched to screaming point.

Her tongue darted out to moisten dry lips. 'What other reason could you have?'

'You work it out.'

'Don't play games with me, Reid. From what I read in the papers, you haven't gone short of female companionship, so it can't be that.'

His eyes narrowed dangerously. 'You shouldn't believe everything you read in the papers. But it isn't your...' there was the slightest pause '...companionship I wanted. I came to offer you a job.'

Relief warred with disappointment inside her. She should be pleased he didn't want to rekindle their relationship, yet she couldn't help the sensation of regret which lanced through her. 'I already have

my work,' she rejoined, hoping he wouldn't notice
the let-down in her voice.

'What I have in mind won't conflict with your
other assignments. Your letter on Suzie's behalf
gave me an idea. I'm snowed under with fan mail
and requests of one sort or another which need
diplomatic replies. You're the person to handle
them.'

She had never felt less diplomatic in her life.
'Don't you have Tonia Rigg for that sort of thing?'

'Tonia has her hands full as my administrative
assistant. In the US I had an agency to handle the
mail but here, I want to try a more personal
approach.'

'So you want me to do the donkey work so Tonia
doesn't have to do it?'

She could have bitten her tongue off as she heard
the suggestion of jealousy in her question. She hated
to give him the idea that it mattered to her one way
or the other. But it was too late.

He fixed her with a sharp look. 'You two never
did get on, did you?'

It was hardly surprising, given their common
interest in one man, who had remained blissfully
blind to the intensity of the rivalry sparking between them. 'It hardly matters now, does it?' she
replied blandly. 'In case you haven't noticed, un-
employment soared while you were overseas empire-
building. You can have your pick of people to
handle your mail. Why choose me?'

'You've apparently forgotten how well we work
together. You were always on my wavelength.

Sometimes I couldn't tell which copy you'd drafted and which I wrote myself.'

Then how come they weren't on the same wavelength when it came to the accident? she thought miserably. He hadn't been able to see how important it was to have him give her the benefit of the doubt. They had been completely out of tune then and nothing of consequence had changed. 'It won't work,' she denied. 'I'm happier working from home than in someone's office.'

He gestured dismissively. 'There's no reason for you to change your arrangements.'

'You'd have the work sent to me?'

'I'll bring it personally if it will convince you to take the job.'

The idea of having him as a client, even on the most innocuous of bases, was enough to shock her out of her lethargy. How could she even consider working with him on any terms? It was bad enough to have him involved in Suzie's music. Now she was actually contemplating a working relationship. She must be crazy.

'No, I . . . it wouldn't be a good idea.'

'Because something of what we shared is still there? That's it, isn't it, Penny?'

It couldn't be possible, could it? Even as her mind screamed a denial, the fine hairs lifted on the back of her neck as if he had caressed her. She took refuge in annoyance. 'Of all the arrogant assumptions. You've been away for nearly five years. For all you know I could have married and had a brood of children in that time.'

His appraising look was more amused than bothered by her assertion. 'Have you done any of those things?'

She wondered why she had chosen such a rash way to try to put some emotional distance between them. Once she had dreamed of marrying Reid and having his children but his own lack of trust in her had ended those hopes. 'Of course not,' she snapped, more annoyed with herself for letting him get to her, than with his response. 'I've been too busy re-establishing myself on the advertising scene in Sydney.'

'Too busy for love? Isn't it rather a waste of what I recall were considerable talents?'

She felt her face flood with colour and busied herself stirring sugar she didn't take into coffee she had no intention of drinking. She'd had no such talent that she'd known about, until his expert tutelage had brought forth passions which would have shocked her if not for his reassurance that what they did was not only natural, it was wonderfully right.

'You seem very sure my—talents, as you call them—have been allowed to go to waste because I've been busy working,' she said with a touch of defensiveness. 'Perhaps I just haven't made as many headlines as you have.'

A thunderous look clouded his expression. 'So there *are* other men in your life, or is it one man, singular?'

She winced inwardly at the implied confirmation of the newspaper stories. His ready acceptance of her lie told her he *had* been involved with a succession of women. Well what did she expect? He was rich, famous and devastatingly attractive. She just hadn't expected the discovery to hurt so much. 'It's hardly any of your business, is it?' she stated, shocked by the ragged state of her nerves. How could she survive working with him if a brief encounter could reduce her to such an emotional wreck?

He surprised her by nodding. 'You're right, it isn't. Nevertheless, I hate to see you struggling when there's something I can do about it.'

So the job offer was no more than charity on his part. He felt sorry for her. A bitter taste filled her mouth. 'I think you'd better go now. If you want to work with Suzie on her music, the school has a programme you should follow. It won't take up much of your time.'

'Or bring me back to your doorstep,' he concluded shrewdly. 'Unfortunately, you force me to decline Suzie's request.'

Her shocked gaze flew to his face. 'For heaven's sake, why? Because I won't work for you ... or because I disappointed you five years ago and this is your way of getting revenge?'

His expression hardened, the shadowed planes and angles so flint-like that she could see why he was such a powerful force in the business world. When he wanted to be, he was made of granite. 'Revenge has nothing to do with this. I checked out the school's mentor programme before I came here. It's a superficial scheme which might bring reflected glory from a few celebrities to the school, but is not designed to give the students any in-depth involvement.'

'The school doesn't expect in-depth involvement. If they did, they'd never get support from people with busy careers. The programme gives the students role models and encouragement. It isn't expected to produce miracles.'

'You know the saying about miracles taking a little longer. If a closer tie with the student is what it takes, I'm prepared to put in the time and energy, but I won't do less. It's an all-or-nothing proposition, Penny. Which is it to be?'

Her hands clawed the air. 'Shouldn't you take this up with Suzie's parents? They'll be back next month. Any decisions will have to involve them anyway.'

His level gaze challenged her. 'I never intended otherwise. But in the meantime, I can make a real difference to Suzie's musical development. It's time she'll never regain if it's allowed to slip by.'

He was pushing her into a corner and her panic grew. 'This is blackmail, making me work for you in return for agreeing to help Suzie.'

Impatience clouded his dark gaze. 'See it how you will. But if you don't take the job, what will you do while I'm working with your niece? It makes more sense to kill two birds with one stone.'

She hadn't thought of it like that. Maybe she was the one getting things out of proportion, allowing her heart to rule her head. She really had no business turning down a lucrative assignment when the house needed so much money spent on it. And it would keep her occupied whenever Reid visited them.

Penny could gracefully resign from Reid's employ once Suzie's parents returned. Surely he wouldn't renege on his commitment to the teenager then? 'All right,' she said in a voice barely above a whisper. 'I'll give it a try, but if it doesn't work out...'

There was a glint of purpose in his expression. No wonder. As usual, his will had prevailed in the end. 'It will work out,' he assured her. 'My plans normally do.'

Penny swallowed hard. Her churning stomach and moist palms were a foretaste of what she could expect when they began to work together. Somehow she would have to get through it for Suzie's sake. It was only for a month, for goodness' sake. She could survive a month, couldn't she? 'When do you want me to start on the letters?' she asked, her tone infuriatingly husky.

'In a few days. We're still getting the building up and functioning. Tonia can manage for the rest of this week until her workload gets up to speed. You looked as if you were heading off for a walk when I joined you. Why don't we continue it and you can show me what's been happening at Kangaluma.'

She slid her palms down the sides of her jeans. 'I mustn't detain you. I gather you're a busy man these days, with a whole building of your own at North Sydney.'

His look was speculative, making her wish she hadn't made it so obvious that she was aware of his progress. 'It has a twin in Los Angeles,' he told

her. 'As well as recording studios in several other
locations. But it's no good being the boss unless
you can escape occasionally. Like now, for
instance.'

As she retreated into silence, he led the way back
to the garden. This time she saw the house as he
must surely see it, the corrugated iron roofing
sagging where it joined the tiled portions of roof,
guttering blocked and leaking, walls cracked, wiring
and plumbing in dire need of replacement.

The only area deserving her pride was the floor
of tesselated tiles in the hallway. Working with an
angle grinder and spirits of salts, she had pains-
takingly cleaned every individual tile. Their rich
colours glowed in the sunlight spilling through the
stained glass panelling of the door and surrounds.

She was sure Reid missed nothing as his assessing gaze covered every inch of their passage.
'There's still a lot more I want to do,' she said,
trying not to sound apologetic. This was her home.
Whether she kept it in good repair or allowed it to
fall down around her ears had nothing to do with
him.

'Your father had to let a lot of things go when
he became ill.' It wasn't a question. The answer was
all too obvious.

'Tell me something I don't know,' she muttered
under her breath.

He reached the end of the teardrop-shaped car-
riage loop which was now grassed over but some
day should be gravelled again, and spun around.
Beyond the loop, a long crescent-shaped bed of

oleanders, roses and red japonica begged to be rescued from the invading couch grass. She should have made time somehow to tidy up the beds.

But he showed no interest in the garden. His focus was on the house silhouetted against the picturesque busyness of Neutral Bay. The building stood on a rise looking across the bay to Garden Island and beyond to Darling Point. It was a million-dollar view if one had the means to bring the property up to standard.

She hated him to see it like this, to see her like this, down at heel. Suddenly she felt as shabby as the garden beds, her hair in sore need of a professional's touch, her face bare of make-up and her old clothes fit only for working at home behind closed doors.

What had happened to the trendy young copywriter he probably remembered? Worn down by her father's illness and the mountain of debts left from his medical care, then from the property itself. Fashionable clothes had come a poor second to keeping her head above water.

How different would things have been if she'd stayed with Reid? Instead of using up her savings on those years overseas, she would have travelled with him as his wife. Kangaluma would have become one of his homes dotted around the globe, no doubt restored to its former glory.

Anger pushed away the sigh which trembled on her lips. They hadn't married for good reason so there was no point dwelling on might-have-beens.

'Have you seen what you wanted to see?' she asked, her tone tremulous.

'Oh, yes.' His gaze lingered on her for a long time until her tension grew unbearably. Every nerve-ending telegraphed the instant, agonising awareness of his maleness, reawakening memories of what they had shared in the past. Might share again in the future?

No! She had to clench her jaw to keep from saying it aloud. Never again would she allow him to trample on her pride. She didn't want his forgiveness and he hadn't earned hers.

'The sea breeze is cool. I'd like to go back inside. You found your way in easily enough. I trust you can see yourself out?'

He inclined his magnificently sculpted head ever so slightly, conceding her attempt at a dignified dismissal. 'I can, as soon as one item of business is resolved.'

What else could there possibly be? 'Can't it wait until I start working for you?'

'No. It concerns the house. I want it.'

Coldness invaded her limbs, but more from an elemental sense of fear than from the cooling breeze off the ocean. 'Kangaluma isn't for sale at any price.'

'Hardly surprising considering the obvious sacrifices you've made to hang on to it. I'm interested in leasing it as a base until I find something more permanent nearby.'

'It's totally unsuitable. You can see how much repair work needs doing.'

He gestured dismissively. 'It can all be taken care of, at my expense of course, since it would be for my benefit.'

How easy he made it sound. It probably was easy, given the vast resources at his disposal. She felt a momentary pang at having to refuse. 'I can't. I don't want to live anywhere else.'

'Who said anything about you living elsewhere?'

Shock coiled through her, closing her throat until she swallowed convulsively. 'You can't mean us to share the house?'

'Why not? We've shared hotel suites before, without even using all the bedrooms as I recall.' There was an edge to his voice which made her want to lash out at him.

'We shared more than a bed then. We shared a trust which no amount of money can restore.'

'You're sure it's beyond repair?'

As long as he believed she was capable of endangering lives, her own and other's, by drinking and driving, there was only one answer. 'Yes. I never want to be involved with you again. You've forced me into a working relationship. You can't force me to share my house with you.'

'The guest wing will suffice for the moment, and I'm prepared to pay well for the use of it.' He named a rental figure which sent her reeling back against a tree in shock.

'That's an outrageous amount and you know it.'

'If necessary, I'll double it to get what I want.'

Her dream of restoring Kangaluma and opening it as a prestige guest lodge sparkled tantalisingly before her eyes. With the kind of money he was offering it was not only possible, she could reach out and touch it. She turned bewildered eyes to him. 'Why Kangaluma? Your budget would get you any property in Sydney.'

'This one is special. It appeals to me for the same reasons it holds you hostage: its long history, its beauty and feeling of permanence. I'm sick to death of hotels and penthouse flats. Kangaluma is a home.'

She could feel herself wavering. Was this how it felt to have the devil make an offer for your soul? 'You're forgetting, it's *my* home. How can I live here while you're here?'

'You will have to oversee the renovations since I won't have much time. Nor do I have your knowledge of the house's history.' His mouth tightened. 'Living in the guest wing, I believe I can manage to restrain myself sufficiently that your honour will be safe if that's what's on your mind.'

Hectic colour raged across her features. How did he know that she was imagining the two of them together? Her heart felt painfully constricted. Hadn't she learned anything from the lessons of the past? If her thoughts were so traitorous at the very idea of sharing a house with him, what would the reality do to her?

Nothing, because she wouldn't allow it. She was committed to working with him and to his involvement with Suzie's music. What difference could it make if he was under their roof as well? He was too busy to spend much time here, and when he found his own house she would have Kangaluma back, and the funds to restore it to its former glory. She would be a fool to pass up all that he was offering simply because of a relationship that was long dead and buried.

'We'll do it your way,' she conceded, feeling her heart begin to pick up speed as she said the words. She set her jaw. 'I have one condition, though.'

His glittering look told her he could afford to be magnanimous since he had achieved everything he wanted. 'Name it.'

'I don't want Tonia Rigg moving in here. I especially don't want...' she licked her lips, her nerve almost going as he regarded her with laser-like intensity ' ... her sleeping here.' With you, she might as well have added with a flash of insight. She didn't like Tonia, but she was civilised enough to tolerate the other woman's presence on business. She shied away from asking herself why she couldn't stand the thought of Reid and Tonia together at Kangaluma.

She wasn't jealous of Tonia, she told herself. Jealousy implied that she still cared for Reid, which certainly wasn't the case. It was just that she...what? She could hardly take the high moral ground and say she disapproved of them sleeping together. A shudder shook her. She didn't, did she? It was...a bad example for Suzie, she decided.

His cynical expression made her wonder how accurately he'd divined her thoughts. 'Tonia has her own place and will continue to run things at North

Sydney,' he assured her. 'Does that satisfy your condition?'

'I suppose so.' A mounting sense of panic took hold. What on earth had she agreed to? She opened her mouth to renege but he was too fast.

'Then it's settled. I'll be back first thing tomorrow to get things moving here.'

CHAPTER FOUR

THE traffic was heavy along Ben Boyd Road as Reid headed back to North Sydney where a mountain of work awaited him. He had stayed longer than he intended at Kangaluma and he would pay for it in late hours tonight. But it was better than returning to the lonely penthouse above his office. Settling into the old house at Neutral Bay was a lot more appealing.

Still mentally attuned to driving on the American side of the road, he had to concentrate to avoid making stupid mistakes, but it didn't stop him thinking about what could be done with the old house.

The biggest stumbling block was its beautiful owner. He hadn't been prepared for the rush of emotion which hit him when he saw Penny Sullivan again. He'd thought he was well and truly over her. And he was, blast it. It was probably just some leftover chemical thing causing him to recoil as if he'd been punched at the first sight of her in that ridiculous building she called a folly.

The flimsy structure had framed her like a picture and he'd been foolishly pleased to see she still wore her hair soft and loose around her face with no artificial curl to detract from her classically beautiful features. She was tinier than he remembered and his fingers flexed as if spanning her waist.

53

He could have picked her up as easily as he picked up his favourite bass clarinet. If the truth be admitted, he could probably play her as skilfully too, although the music they would make would be of a very different kind.

He frowned at himself in the driving mirror, calling to mind the reason why they'd split up.

Penny still couldn't understand his obsession with the accident but she hadn't been there the day he saw the wreck of his parents' car on the evening news, watched the sheet-covered bodies being lifted clear. The camera had panned to a police officer interviewing a man who was obviously drunk and crying with remorse. A lot of good his regrets had done for Reid's parents.

No names would be released until the family had been notified, the story had said. That was him, Reid had realised with a sick feeling. At fifteen years old, he was all that was left of his family.

All their plans lay in ruins. His father would never tour with him when he became a famous musician. His mother would never sit in the front row when he debuted at Carnegie Hall. All the love, all the support he'd depended on for fifteen years was gone, wiped out by a fool who was too drunk to understand the tragedy he'd caused.

Reid had never felt so angry at anyone. He was told later he'd kicked in the television screen but he had no memory of it, only of wanting to vent a towering rage on something or someone. His loss could never be redressed. He didn't know if he had it in him to forgive such a terrible wrong. Was it any wonder he had no time for people who drank and drove? He'd expected better of Penny.

Yet she acted as if *he* was the criminal. Hell, he had offered to forgive and forget. Well, all right, maybe to forgive. Having these thoughts meant he was unlikely ever to forget. But if she had only faced up to her mistake instead of looking for someone else to blame, things might have worked out between them.

Because she couldn't remember getting behind the wheel of the car, she expected him to believe she couldn't have done it. It was more likely that she was drunker than she realised.

Her solution had been to run away to England to work. Yet hadn't he done the same himself? No, it wasn't the same, he defended himself mentally. Unlike her, he had nothing to run away from.

Maybe it was a good thing that Suzie's letter had brought them together. He had wanted a home and it wasn't until he'd seen Kangaluma again that he'd realised it was *that* home he wanted. He hadn't been entirely honest with Penny about buying another place nearby. He wanted Kangaluma and he meant to have it, one way or another.

If it meant sharing with her for a while, so be it, although if today's reaction was any guide he'd have to watch his step. The thing with Penny was over and he had no plans to start such a thankless involvement again.

All the same, seeing the house come back to life was going to be a challenge he welcomed. His mind raced ahead. He knew just the builder for the job, a man who specialised in restoring heritage buildings. When the price was right the man could move mountains.

Reid reached for his car phone.

'Isn't this totally awesome?'

Watching the tradesmen parading through her house, Penny was forced to agree, but her definition of 'awesome' was closer to her dictionary's—inspiring of dread.

When Reid had said he meant to make a few changes to the house for his own convenience she had assumed he meant new paint and carpeting in the rooms he planned to use. She had never dreamed he meant practically to rebuild Kangaluma around her.

She should have smelled a rat when Reid had arrived with an architect in tow but he had summarily dismissed her while he showed the woman over the property. The builder had arrived two weeks ago armed with plans which he spread all over the dining-room table.

Penny hadn't minded having her work area relocated to a room at the back of the house if it was only for a few days. But as the construction noise, dust and paint smells increased, so did her annoyance. Whose house did Reid Branden think this was?

The answer was disturbingly obvious, she thought, glimpsing his jacket slung over a chair beyond her open door. His books were piled beside hers on the coffee-table and his choice of coffee—Mocha Kenya, she recalled wryly—had supplanted her instant brand in the kitchen.

It wasn't just the physical signs of his presence which bothered her, she was forced to admit. She hadn't counted on the enormous emotional cost of sharing the house with him. Even when he wasn't here, he was—haunting her thoughts, bringing back memories.

A picnic in Centennial Park and horseriding afterwards. Reid on a magnificent bay, a knight without his armour...

Holding hands as they sat on a rug listening to Joan Sutherland sing Donizetti's *Lucia di Lammermoor* under the stars while Reid hummed in time under his breath...

Sailing across Sydney Harbour in a friend's yacht, Reid at the helm, his hair caught by the wind, his eyes bright with enthusiasm....

Stop it, she implored herself. This was getting her nowhere. She looked down at her hands. They were trembling.

She was trying to come to grips with some of his vast pile of mail—and this was only three days' worth—when a man stuck his head around the door. 'Could get a bit noisy around here today, love. The guest bathroom's going in behind the panelling in the hall. Just thought I'd warn you.'

Guest bathroom? Panelling? Enough was enough. Shutting down her computer, she threw a dust cover over it and stood up. 'I'll be going out anyway.'

He nodded approvingly. 'Best thing you could do.'

She wondered if Reid would agree when she bearded him in his office as soon as she'd dropped

Suzie off at school. The teenager began to protest that she wasn't a child, she could take the bus with her friends, but one look at Penny's thunderous face silenced her. 'I'll get my bag.'

It was Penny's first visit to the concrete and glass edifice which housed Reid's company and she was taken aback by the size and complexity of it. Knowing Reid had done well and being confronted with the evidence were horses of different colours. His name and company logo gleamed at her well before she drove into the underground car park.

'This space is reserved for Mr Branden,' the attendant told her haughtily, gesturing at the name stencilled at the head of a space big enough for three cars. She had already recognised Reid's Mercedes in one slot.

She favoured the attendant with a saccharine smile. 'It's OK. We live together.'

Leaving him open-mouthed, she flounced towards a bank of lifts and took out some of her pent-up emotion on the buttons identifying the executive floor. The door slid open on to a reception area which was the last word in opulence.

The sight of so much marble and chrome, plush carpeting and state-of-the-art limewashed furnishings almost undermined her resolve. What was she doing here? Then she remembered. She had business to discuss with Reid, and where better to do it than in his business setting?

Two levels of secretaries later she found herself in Tonia Rigg's office, which would have housed the managing director in many organisations. Penny wrinkled her nose. What had she been missing by staying out of the workforce for so long?

Tonia's teeth smiled as she recognised Penny. 'It's been a long time, Penny...Sullivan, isn't it?'

As if the name weren't engraved on her memory. According to Tonia, Penny's drunken driving had almost killed her. It was an effort to smile back. 'Hello, Tonia. You're looking as stunning as ever. Don't tell me you succumbed to the American fashion for cosmetic surgery?'

To Tonia's credit she kept her temper, although sparks flashed in her green cat's-eyes. 'Are you speaking from experience? Because it isn't something the women in my family need to worry about so I wouldn't know.'

Touché, Penny thought, knowing she'd asked for it. Somehow Tonia managed to bring out the worst in her. She conceded the round and asked almost meekly, 'Is Reid in? I need to see him about the work he's having done at my house.'

'Ah, yes, he's living in your guest wing temporarily.' She emphasised the last word.

Penny felt herself slipping. 'What makes you think he's in the guest wing? I have a lovely queen-sized bed in my suite.'

The assertion startled Tonia but also Penny herself. The other woman paled but recovered quickly. 'Your house is a novelty to Reid. He enjoys turning sows' ears into silk purses. You should have seen what he did with a near-derelict antebellum mansion in the American south. Naturally, once the project's complete we'll move on to something else.'

Tonia's use of the plural was surprisingly distressing but Penny masked her reaction. She had made her decision five years ago, painful though it had been. All the same she wondered whether Reid had moved in with the owner of the antebellum mansion until he restored it.

Reminded of her purpose, she asked, 'Will you tell Reid I'm here?'

A frosty smile thwarted her. 'He's in conference at present and can't be interrupted.'

Penny debated the wisdom of barging in on Reid. Several doors opened off Tonia's office with no clues as to which one led to Reid. 'I'll wait,' she decided finally.

'It could be a while, but suit yourself. Would you like coffee, or something stronger?'

The oblique reference to Penny's supposed taste for alcohol was almost the last straw. No wonder Reid was so attached to Tonia. They were probably the only people who measured up to Reid's perfectionist standards. She took a breath. 'I don't need anything, thank you.'

Tonia inclined her head. 'Perhaps a magazine, then? *Business Week* might suit, since *Vogue* doesn't seem to be your thing.'

All right, so Penny's long black skirt and loosely woven cream sweater had seen better days, but she'd thrown them on to confront Reid, not to dazzle him with her fashion sense. Although, looking at Tonia's gorgeous beige wool suit and frilled salmon blouse, Penny wondered if she'd been wise. Perhaps he'd take her more seriously if she presented a more glossy image.

Darn it, what was going on here? Slightly bohemian was her style. Why was it suddenly a problem because Reid was back? She set her jaw and reached for a copy of the literary magazine, *Quadrant*. Clothes did not make the man, or woman for that matter.

Tonia didn't take the hint and return to work. 'I suppose you thought it was clever, hooking Reid's interest with that fake letter from your niece?'

Penny's eyes blazed. 'It was not fake. Suzie is a talented musician and the mentor programme is important to her.'

Tonia's expression was dubious. 'Yet you aren't worried about her reputation?'

'What do you mean?'

'Reid's reputation is not exactly saintly when it comes to women. Aren't you afraid he'll tarnish your niece's private-school image by association?'

'It's hardly an association. He's only giving Suzie the benefit of his professional expertise. Where's the harm in that?'

Tonia sniffed. 'Well, don't say I didn't warn you.'

Suspicion darkened Penny's gaze, but the other woman's face was impassive. It wasn't like Tonia to worry about someone else's reputation so what was she up to?

Penny had no time to worry about it because one of the doors opened and a group of businessmen stepped out, talking earnestly. Reid's eyebrows lifted when he saw her but he waited until he had escorted his guests to the lift before he addressed her.

'To what do I owe this visit?'

Penny glanced at Tonia. 'I need to talk to you—privately.'

'Very well, we'll talk over lunch.'

'No, I'd rather...'

But what she'd rather do was overruled by the pressure of his hand on her arm as he steered her to the lift. 'Do you still like Italian food?'

'Yes, but...'

'I have a standing reservation at the Piccolo at Milson's Point.'

She stifled her objections at the mention of the stylish restaurant which overlooked Sydney Harbour. Maybe she could consider the lunch a kind of penalty on Reid for riding roughshod over her home life.

The restaurant had an unprepossessing façade and was hidden behind a modern office tower. Once inside, however, she was faced with a panoramic view of the harbour from a wall of windows, open today to admit the gentle sea breezes and the glorious spring sunshine.

Reid's table was alongside a window and the breeze fanned her face. She opted for Perrier water to drink and an entrée of king prawns followed by char-grilled balmain bugs.

Reid handed the menu to the waiter. 'I'll have the same.' He leaned towards her. 'Now, what was so pressing it couldn't wait until tonight?'

She'd been wrong. This was far too intimate a setting for the stern lecture she'd prepared. 'The renovations,' she began, 'they're too much. You have to stop.'

He paused to sample their wine and nodded his approval, waiting until it was poured before he answered. 'If it's the money, I'm paying for them since they're for my benefit.'

'That's beside the point. I thought you meant paint and carpet. When I left, ten carpenters were repanelling my hall with faithfully reproduced cedar panelling and four plumbers were busy concealing a bathroom behind it.'

'Aren't you happy with the standard of workmanship?'

'No. I mean, of course I'm happy with it. It's a work of art. But that's the problem. I can't afford to live in a work of art.'

Their prawns arrived and he began to work on his while hers lay untouched in front of her. 'You're not making a lot of sense.'

She began to explain about her father leaving the house to herself and Jo while allowing her to live in it as long as she needed to, ending with her dream of buying Jo out eventually. 'At the rate you're going I'll never be able to afford it,' she finished. 'You're making it much too valuable.'

Having unburdened herself, she began to peel the prawns and found them surprisingly tasty. Misery always gave her an appetite.

Reid played with his wine glass. 'Why didn't you tell me this before?'

'I would have done if I'd known you meant to do so much.'

He thought for a moment, staring out at the hive of activity that was the site of the old Luna Park below them. It reminded her of her home. 'The solution's obvious.'

'You'll call off your army of workers?'

'No. I'll tell them to hold off until I can get the place professionally valued as is. Then the renovations won't be taken into account when deciding how much Jo's half is worth, because I'll own them.'

'Is that possible?'

'Anything's possible if you're sufficiently determined.'

It was a bonus he hadn't expected. His solution would give him a stake in Kangaluma long before he'd anticipated it. Persuading Penny to sell the place to him should be easier than ever once she acknowledged his stake in the property.

The possibility had already occurred to her, he saw from the anger staining her cheeks with red. 'It only means I'll have two of you to repay. How is that supposed to help?'

'Haven't you heard the saying—where there's a will, there's a way?'

But it was usually his will and his way, she also remembered. She tensed as their main course was served. Why hadn't she ordered something they wouldn't have to share? The balmain bugs, more like miniature lobsters, were served on the half-shell, in a huge mound between them. Since they were best eaten with the fingers, there was no way she could avoid brushing his hand when they reached across at the same moment.

He was the one who pulled back, she noticed with a sick feeling. However civilised he might behave towards her, he still didn't respect her, didn't even want to touch her.

'You haven't touched your wine,' he pointed out.

'These days I rarely do.' Her car was at North Sydney and she still had to drive home. No matter what he thought, she didn't mix drinking and driving.

She was barely aware of what he talked about during the meal, being much too conscious of every move and gesture he made. It was like a parody of the meals they had shared before...making her ache for the small pleasures now lost to her. His instinctive pulling away from her stayed in her mind. Did she really disgust him so much that he resented even the accidental touch of her hand? Then why was he so determined to share Kangaluma with her?

She remembered the antebellum mansion. Was the challenge of restoring the house what mattered to him? Maybe he wouldn't care if she moved out altogether.

After coffee, he signalled for their bill and settled it, adding a tip which made her wince, further emphasising the gulf which now separated them. He moved her chair back. 'Do you have to collect Suzie from school?'

She shook her head. 'She prefers to come on the bus with her friends. I was in her bad books this morning because I insisted on dropping her off.'

'Then we can go straight to the house.'

We? She hadn't planned on going anywhere with him. The lunch had already strained her endurance more than she would have thought possible. 'But we can't. My car's parked at your building.'

'Give me the keys and I'll have it driven over for you. You want this valuation under way as soon as possible, don't you?'

'I do, but...'

'Good. Let's go.'

Once again she was carried along by his irresistible sense of purpose. Had he always been like this, a tidal force which carried others along in his wake? Yes, she acknowledged as they drove back to Neutral Bay. From their first encounter he had exerted a magnetic pull over her which was impossible to resist. She had always assumed she hadn't wanted to, but it was a resolve she had never tried to test. Now she wondered whether it would have made any difference.

Oh, he wouldn't have forced her to do anything against her will. Rape or anything remotely like it wasn't in his vocabulary. But he was quite capable of persuading her that she didn't really want to refuse him. Taking no for an answer wasn't his style.

He'd done it again over lunch, she realised, sneaking a sidelong glance at him as he drove. She'd stormed into his office determined to make him stop working on her house. Yet somehow he had got his own way. How had it happened? She wasn't at all sure.

Looking at him was a mistake, she realised. It made her all too aware of the strength of his profile as he concentrated on the traffic. His musician's hands rested easily on the steering-wheel and each time they stopped at the lights they tapped out a rhythm he must be hearing in his head.

She swallowed hard, reminded in spite of herself of the feel of those hands playing delicious melodies of love up and down her spine. A tingling ran through her at the thought and she shuddered slightly. If music be the food of love...

No, she told herself. They were too far out of tune ever to make that kind of music again. All she had to do was remember his expression when he touched her by accident in the restaurant. The fleeting glimpse of his shock and disgust was proof of what he thought of her. They might work together, might even become friends of a sort, but underneath the veneer would lie the sickening truth. He despised everything about her.

She stared bleakly at the road ahead. Why did it always come back to the same thing? He thought she was capable of risking lives, including her own, by drinking and driving, while she was convinced she was not. Where did her certainty come from when all the evidence was against it?

She rammed the heel of her hand against her forehead. Why couldn't she recall exactly what had happened that night five years ago? Then she could either accept her own guilt or be exonerated. Was she really trying to deny her actions? Reid thought so, and it was the main bone of contention between them.

'Headache?' he enquired.

She let her hand drop. 'No, just thinking.'

Thankfully he didn't pursue the question and they soon arrived at Kangaluma where Reid began issuing orders. Within a short time, the tradesmen were packing up their tools, although Reid assured

her they would be back as soon as the valuation
was completed.

'This is only a minor hitch.'

Like hell, she couldn't help thinking. She had expected him to return to work once he'd arranged
the valuation but he seemed in no hurry to leave.
'Suzie will be back soon. I can spend some time
working with her,' he explained in response to
Penny's slightly impatient query.

Suddenly she became aware that they were alone
in the house for the first time. The tradesmen had
gone and Suzie wasn't due home yet. A sense of
near-panic flashed through her. Yet she wasn't
afraid of him. It was more an—awareness—as if
every nerve-ending she possessed had gone on full
alert.

Unknowingly she shifted slightly away. 'Would
you like me to make some coffee?'

His level gaze mocked her. 'No, thank you.'

This was impossible. She couldn't behave like a
polite stranger around him, and there was nothing
else she could be to him any more. She flicked construction dust from a pile of books on a counter-
top but it settled back again. 'What would you like,
then?'

'I could think of several things but none of them
would be given willingly, would they, Penny?'

She tossed her head defiantly to mask the turmoil
inside her. 'If you mean would I sleep with you,
you're right, I'd rather die.'

A taunting smile broadened his sensuous mouth.
'You weren't always so negative about my
attentions.'

You weren't always so negative about me, she thought furiously, but stifled the retort. In any war of words he would always win. For someone who made her living with words Penny found it almost impossible to use them as weapons. Perhaps she was too conscious of their power to wound beyond healing.

But there were times, such as now, when she wished she could fully express her antagonism towards him. Sharing coffee with her was about as close as he would ever get again.

'You never did tell me whether there's anyone special in your life,' he went on in a drawl which suggested he knew precisely what she was thinking.

'Yes, I did. I said it was none of your business and your moving in here hasn't changed my response.'

He slanted her a look of wry amusement. 'Oh, but it has. No man worthy of the name would allow another man to move in on his territory. Your agreement was all the answer I needed.'

'Damn you, Reid. Why did you insist on living here?' She gestured at the building chaos around them. 'It can't be because of the ambience. Your secretary's office has more atmosphere than this house right now. So why are you doing this?'

Cynical amusement darkened his eyes. 'You know what they say about the other man's grass?'

'And what about when you find out it isn't any greener on this side of the fence?'

His frankly assessing look played havoc with her composure, making her want to turn and run rather than endure another moment of this conversation.

But his eyes held her in thrall. 'So far it's very green indeed.'

She shook her head. 'You're imagining things.'

He took several steps closer. 'Far from it. My years of performing have enabled me to read an audience until I almost know what they're thinking.' He moved closer still. 'I *always* know what they want.'

A lump rose in her throat and she swallowed hard, feeling her pulsebeat quicken. 'This time you're wrong. I accepted your help with the house but it doesn't mean I want anything more from you.'

His finger grazed the side of her face, sending tremors surging along her spine. Her heart almost stopped as she remembered other moments like this which had ended in a crescendo of feverish love-making. Those moments had started with a touch, too. A shudder shook her but she wasn't sure whether it was of rejection or... something more dangerous.

'Are you sure?' he murmured. Sweeping her hair aside, he bent to kiss the nape of her neck and the room rocked around her. She had forgotten how compelling his kiss could feel against her fevered skin. Her breathing gathered speed.

How easy it would be to give in, to let him carry her to the bedroom and satisfy her body's yearnings which had gone unanswered for so long. What a fool she was to think she had buried them for good. His mere touch was all it took to make a liar of her.

She was aware of the need to do something, anything to end this before it reached its logical conclusion, but her muscles refused to obey her commands. When he lowered his head and probed the sensitive corner of her mouth with his lips, she gave a groan which was half protest, half capitulation.

'You see,' he murmured against her mouth, the vibration reaching her very soul, 'I can still read my audience accurately.'

There was mocking laughter in his voice as he stepped away from her. Anger boiled through her, as much at herself for proving him right as at him for daring to touch her.

Daring? She had practically invited him, she derided herself, feeling the colour flood her face. 'You bastard,' she snapped. 'It was a mistake to let you share this house, no matter how much I needed the money. I should have known you'd take advantage of the situation.'

Unmoved by her anger, he gave a throaty chuckle. 'Ah, but you *did* know,' he said with infuriating certainty. 'You just don't want to admit it to yourself.'

CHAPTER FIVE

ANGRY denial exploded through her. There was no
way she had planned or even hoped he would kiss
her. She didn't want anything to do with a man
who regarded her with contempt to the point of
avoiding accidental contact with her.

He hadn't shied away this time, she thought with
a slight shock. He had kissed her with all the fire
and passion at his command, and she had responded...oh, how she had responded. It galled her
to think of it, knowing she should have thrust him
away at the first touch of those sensuous lips.

Why hadn't she? She wouldn't allow that he was
right, that she wanted him to take advantage of her.
His look said he knew what she was thinking and
the corners of his mouth turned up with
satisfaction.

'I suppose you think it's amusing to force
yourself on a woman,' she flung at him in furious
rebellion against her own feelings.

'On the contrary. I don't find force amusing in
any context, especially the sexual one. Nor was any
such thing necessary a moment ago. The strongest
pressure I used was a finger crooked under your
chin like this.'

He demonstrated, and a shudder rippled through
her from head to toe before she jerked her head

aside. 'How could I ever have made the mistake of thinking I loved you?'

'We all make mistakes,' he said evenly. 'Some of us are more willing to admit to them than others.'

There was no mistaking his meaning. Her refusal to admit to driving his car on the night of the accident was a denial of responsibility. What would happen if she capitulated? Would her *mea culpa* bring absolution in the form of his love?

If so, was it such a giant step to take? She was terribly afraid she *was* to blame and, in the absence of other evidence, what other explanation was there? But something held her back from the admission. 'No,' her lips formed soundlessly. Not even for the ecstasy she had glimpsed in his arms could she trade her belief that there was more to be known about the events of that night.

His eyebrows arched upwards. 'Still no? It's your favourite word lately, Penny.'

'I find it's the best defence where you're concerned.'

His eyes shifted rapidly from blue to an angry sea-green. 'Even the most impregnable defences can be breached.'

She spread her hands helplessly. 'Why would you want to?'

'A question I've been asking myself from the moment I set eyes on you in that damned folly.'

So she was a challenge to him, the one that got away. She should have remembered how single-minded he could be. But she had never dreamed she would be the focus of his determination. Suddenly she felt more vulnerable than at any time since they parted. 'What do you really want from me?' she asked on a note of despair.

'Besides the obvious? I want Kangaluma.'

'My house?' The question came out as a strained whisper.

'It's only half yours. I want to buy you and Jo out and make this my permanent home.'

Her eyes widened in shock. 'All the work you're having done . . . you planned this from the first, didn't you?'

'It must be obvious that no one invests this kind of money in a rental proposition.'

But to be scheming to take her home from her . . . it was too much. 'You can't, I won't let you,' she vowed, hearing her voice tremble with emotion.

'It's too late. If I withdraw my financial support you'll have no choice but to put the property to auction and I'll make sure I'm the highest bidder. Or you can sell to me at the unrenovated valuation and the timing will be up to you.'

Hysterical laughter bubbled in her throat. 'You must hate me a great deal.'

He looked genuinely surprised. 'I don't hate you at all, Penny. This is purely a business proposition. I'm probably doing you a favour.'

'How do you work that out?'

'This place is far too big for a single woman to manage on her own. You should be socialising more, not spending your weekends fighting the war of the weeds.'

'So now you're an expert on my love-life as well? Thanks for your concern but I'd rather be left alone with my weeds.'

He shook his head. 'I'd be doing you a great disservice if I allowed it. Of course, there is another possibility.'

'I can hardly wait to hear.'

'We could share Kangaluma on a permanent basis.'

Tension thrummed through her. 'You mean live together?'

'Exactly. You'd never want for anything again.'

'And you'd have a live-in plaything whenever your libido demanded it, right?'

Diamond-hard points gleamed in his eyes. 'Is that the deal you're offering?'

She chose her words with care. 'The deal I'm offering is for you to go to hell.'

He seemed unmoved although she was shaking with reaction. 'I much prefer the first option.'

Before she could summon an even more caustic response, they were interrupted by the slamming of the front door and Suzie's cheerful greeting floated through to them. 'In here,' Penny responded in a choked voice, shooting a warning glance at Reid.

Her warning elicited an angry frown at her silent implication that he might involve Suzie in this. Penny felt slightly ashamed. His behaviour towards her niece had been kindness itself. She had no right to assume that he would drag the teenager into their private quarrel.

By the time Suzie walked into the living-room he was standing by the French windows, hands in pockets, looking out towards the bay. Penny kept her distance across the room, her agitation masked by the pleasant smile she gave her niece. 'Hi, Suzie. Good day at school?'

'Average.' Her eyes brightened as she caught sight of Reid. 'Hello. You're home early. Checking on the renovations?'

'I had lunch with your aunt and decided to stick around to do some more mentoring if you're up to it.'

Suzie's face lit up. 'Cool! I'll get my gear.'

'Which tutor are you using?' Reid queried.

'Lazarus, second level. I'm almost on to third.'

He nodded. 'Good, bring them with you.'

'We'll meet you in the folly,' Penny contributed. 'It's too chaotic inside.' And too claustrophobic with Reid in the same room, she acknowledged to herself. Outdoors, she might be able to think more clearly. No matter what he thought, she wasn't giving up Kangaluma so easily.

Once outside, the silence weighed heavily on her. She registered Reid's presence beside her as a dark force, as elemental as a storm-tossed sea and just as implacable. How could she contest such a force and hope to win?

He seemed to read her thoughts. 'This doesn't have to be a contest. Remember my alternative?'

'And my answer,' she threw at him.

'Which was hardly a considered response.'

'If I considered it for the rest of my life it would come out the same,' she voiced vehemently.

'We'll see,' was all he said.

Fortunately Suzie joined them quickly and she and Reid settled down to work in the shady comfort of the folly.

Penny had brought along a clipboard and pen, meaning to draft replies to Reid's letters at the same time. But focusing on the task proved impossible when she was vibrantly aware of him not two metres away. His whole attention was fixed on Suzie's playing and he seemed oblivious of Penny's presence until he glanced up and their eyes met. He knew she'd been watching him, damn him. She made herself concentrate on her work.

Suzie's playing was also a distraction, especially when Reid interrupted her after a few notes. 'The Giampieri should start calmly, like ocean waves lapping the shore, then build to powerful breakers crashing down,' he explained patiently.

Like Reid's kisses, Penny thought distractedly, recalling how his lips had teased her gently, then provoked her to a torrent of tumultuous feelings. The music mocked her as it resonated with her confused feelings.

Unable to endure any more, she stood up. 'I'll fetch us some cold drinks.' She refused Suzie's offer of help. 'The lemonade's already made. It won't take a minute.'

The haunting voice of the clarinet followed her along the path back to the house, distracting her so she almost collided with a harried-looking young man coming the other way. A substantial black leather case swung from one shoulder and he was casually dressed in jeans and a denim battle jacket.

He looked surprised to see her. 'I was told I'd find Reid Branden here,' he said.

'You must be the valuer,' she assumed. 'Mr Branden's in the summerhouse at the end of this path. Just follow the music.'

He looked as if she'd given him a gift. 'Thanks, I will.' He hurried off in the direction she indicated.

Odd man, she thought as she went inside. But then she didn't know much about his profession. Trust Reid to conjure up a valuer so quickly. He must have dropped everything in response to Reid's telephone summons. Typical, she couldn't help thinking. Was she the only one who resented being asked to dance to his tune?

Resignedly she put another glass and extra home-baked shortbreads on to the tray then set off to rejoin the others.

She was almost bowled over by the valuer coming the other way. His case hung open and she glimpsed a long black barrel protruding from it. He gave her a wolfish smile. 'Thanks, lady. You were a big help.'

A big help in what way? Doubts assailed her as she carried the tray to the folly. They were confirmed as soon as she saw Reid's thunderous expression. He set the tray down with such force the glasses rattled, then turned on her. 'Why did you let that scum in here?'

'Wasn't he the valuer you sent for?' She was afraid she already knew the answer.

'Of course he wasn't. He's a Press photographer for *Inside* magazine.'

Her hand went to her mouth. 'Oh, no!'

'Oh, yes. The magazine that prints lurid behind-the-scenes stories about celebrities' lives, and invents what they can't find out any other way.'

She had not only allowed him onto her property, she had told him where to find Reid. 'I didn't know,' she said in a stunned whisper.

'I would hope not, or I'd personally wring your beautiful neck,' he ground out.

'He didn't actually get any photos, did he?'

'Several before I threw him out. These guys shoot and run. Didn't you see the bloody great camera he was carrying?'

'Not until he was leaving. It was hidden in his bag when he arrived.' She turned luminous eyes on him. 'He got you and Suzie together, didn't he?'

Suzie was excitedly unaware of the potential calamity. 'Reid was showing me some fingering when this guy jumped out and snapped our pictures. Are they going to be in a magazine?'

'I'm afraid so.' His tone said he was also afraid this particular magazine wouldn't write anything they'd be happy to read. They'd once called Reid a playboy musician and she could imagine the fun they'd have linking him with the private school's mentor programme. It was the very possibility which Tonia had warned her about.

Tonia!

Penny's heart sank. The secretary must have tipped off the magazine. How else could they have found out about Reid's involvement with the school programme? But without proof that Tonia was behind this, Reid was more likely to believe his trusted assistant. Penny kept her suspicions to herself. 'What are we going to do?' she asked tonelessly.

His mouth set into a grim line. 'The best defence is a good offence, and I intend to start offending right now.'

'How? Even you can't stop a magazine like *Inside* from writing what they choose to.'

'I don't have to. I can provide a story which will push their efforts right out of the headlines.'

'What do you have in mind?'

'The announcement of our engagement.'

She felt as if she'd been poleaxed. 'What?'

Suzie was beside herself with excitement. 'You two are getting engaged? This is so cool.'

It was also impossible. 'Suzie, why don't you take the tray and your things back to the house? Reid and I need to talk.'

With a grudging agreement, Suzie complied. As soon as they were alone, Penny whirled on Reid. 'You must be out of your mind. I'm not marrying you. I'm not getting engaged to you. I hate you, is that simple enough for you?'

'The alternative is to ride out the bad press, but I warn you, it won't be pretty. I couldn't give a damn what they write about me, considering I've given them some fair ammunition over time, but it's hardly fair to involve Suzie's school when it could endanger the whole mentor programme. Is that what you'd rather see happen?'

'Of course not.' What happened to Penny obviously didn't rate his concern. But she couldn't let her niece suffer if she could prevent it. What if the headlines resulted in the whole mentor scheme being shut down? 'Are you sure this is the answer?' she asked.

'If I'm about to become a respectably married man, there's hardly scope for scandal, is there? Provided we put a good enough face on it, we leave them without a leg to stand on and the mentor scheme will be safe.'

What choice did she have? 'Very well, I'll do it, but only for Suzie's sake,' she conceded. 'I know how much this project means to her.'

'Why else would you agree to become engaged to a man you hate?' he queried wryly, then became businesslike. 'I'll need to move fast. *Inside* publishes on a Friday. Today's Tuesday so I'll call a Press conference and make the announcement tomorrow morning. It will be carried by the evening news broadcasts and Thursday morning's papers. By Friday, *Inside* will look like the last horse in the race.'

Her head felt as if it was spinning. How could he be so decisive about something like this? Even if it was only until the threat of scandal passed, there was still the ordeal of a public engagement for Penny to endure. Forever afterwards she'd be the woman who was once engaged to Reid Branden, an object of envy while they were together, then of pity after they separated.

Once upon a time the idea of being engaged to Reid would have been sheer heaven. Now she wasn't sure what she felt. Apprehension certainly. But there was something more, a coiling almost of excitement deep inside her which defied logical explanation.

She couldn't *like* the idea of being publicly proclaimed as his bride-to-be. And she had no in-

tention of taking this any further than absolutely
necessary. All the same, part of her met the challenge almost eagerly. Was this what temporary insanity felt like?

By next morning she was convinced she'd fallen
victim to it as she contemplated the Press conference which Reid had arranged. Gripped by
nervous tension, she couldn't force down a bite of
breakfast.

'You'll feel better if you eat something,' Reid advised. 'Take it from a seasoned performer.'

She shook her head. 'I couldn't. Isn't there some
way you can handle this without me?'

'A wedding without a bride seems rather incom-
plete,' he said with cool detachment.

She turned horror-stricken eyes to him. 'Who said
anything about a bride or a wedding?'

An eyebrow lifted ironically. 'Don't they usually
follow an engagement?'

'Not this time.'

He rose smoothly. 'Then you have nothing to
worry about, have you?'

He called it nothing, she thought, aghast, as they
prepared to enter the boardroom which had been
set up for the Press conference a short time later.
Nervously she smoothed her lace-trimmed sweater
over its matching trumpet-shaped skirt. Both were
in a shade of melon which flattered her colouring
and emphasised her trim figure without drawing too
much attention to it. Or so the boutique assistant
had convinced her in the short time she'd had to
choose a new outfit. Reid had offered to pay for it
but she drew the line at having him purchase clothes

for her. Their engagement wasn't the kind to allow such intimacies. So the investment had stretched her slender budget, further disturbing her equilibrium.

She was glad she had succumbed to temptation when she saw the throng awaiting them in the boardroom. There were at least three television camera crews in evidence and the table where they were to sit was cluttered with microphones and miniature tape recorders. Knowing she looked her best bolstered her courage.

A murmur of interest greeted their arrival. All eyes were on them as Reid escorted her to the table. His arm was firmly around her waist, giving her no choice but to match her steps to his and lean slightly into his embrace.

Every time his hip brushed hers she felt a jolt like electricity arcing through her. His hand curving possessively around her made her feel disturbingly vulnerable, as if he was leading her to something akin to an execution. Well, wasn't it? the thought flashed through her mind. Any semblance of a private life would be destroyed once Reid made his announcement.

He gripped her hand as they took their seats, surprising her by giving it an encouraging squeeze. Then he released her and leaned towards the bank of microphones to welcome the media. His style was elegantly relaxed, making her envy his composure. Of course he was skilled at making public appearances. But he brought a warmth and genuineness to his words which experience alone couldn't account for.

The thought made her want to smile and eased some of her nervous tension. It was as if she was really proud of him, instead of play-acting for the media's benefit. Surely she should focus on how much she disliked him and how furious she was that his presence in her house had gotten her into this predicament?

'I returned to Australia to do two things,' Reid was saying when she forced her attention back to his words. 'The first was to establish my corporate headquarters at North Sydney, and you can see the results around you. The second——' he paused for dramatic effect '—was to ask Penny Sullivan to marry me. Yesterday she did me the honour of accepting.'

A predictable uproar followed his announcement then the journalists began bombarding them with questions.

'How long have you known Miss Sullivan?'

'Is it true the two of you were together before you went overseas?'

'Why did you wait so long to come back and claim her?'

He answered them all good-naturedly, taking his time over the last question. 'The best things in life are worth waiting for. I had a business to build and music to play. Penny was pursuing her writing career. It wasn't until I got back that we realised we didn't want to wait any longer, did we, darling?'

The loving look with which he favoured her as he used the endearment made her face burn. Flashbulbs exploded all over the room, capturing her bridal blushes for posterity. 'No, we didn't want to wait,' she said, choosing her words with care. 'When I met Reid again it was as if we'd never been apart.' The antipathy had been every bit as strong, she added mentally, making the statement true enough in its way.

'What brought the two of you back together?'

'Well, we...'

'It was a letter from a special young lady who will soon become my niece,' he cut in smoothly, sensing her rising panic. 'Suzanne Kimber is a talented young musician who asked me to become her mentor, not realising that I already had the closest possible ties with her family—ties of love.'

The memory of his kiss, so sweetly pleasurable, filled her mind until she reminded herself that his speech was for the media. It took all of her willpower to smile fondly at him and nod in seeming agreement.

'How's about a kiss, Reid?' prompted a television cameraman.

Reid's mouth widened into a megavolt smile which turned Penny's insides to jelly. 'You're hardly my type, Stan,' he joked. 'If you'll settle for me kissing my fiancée, it will be a pleasure.'

Her body tensed at the prospect of being publicly claimed in this way but he seemed unperturbed as he slid a hand along the back of her neck and drew her face to him.

The lingering pressure of his mouth on hers was for the benefit of the cameras, she told herself wildly, but it didn't stop the tension ebbing from her body and a warmth spreading through her like wildfire.

Contrarily, her heart raced and weakness invaded her limbs as his strong arms enveloped her. A shudder shook her, although it didn't seem to match the revulsion she knew she should be feeling. Flashbulbs popped around them. Trying to glare her anger at him for doing this, she was momentarily blinded.

Blinking away the stars which spotted her vision, she was aware of Reid thanking the journalists for their attention. He seemed unaware of her fury, which was as much at herself for letting him manipulate her feelings as at him for staking claim to her so publicly.

It was what they had agreed to, after all, but it didn't stop the humiliation which welled up inside her. Why couldn't she do as he was doing: put on an outward show without it affecting her so powerfully? This was only the beginning. The charade had a long way to go yet.

It was working, Reid saw with satisfaction as he read the headlines over the succeeding week. The photo of him and Suzie had appeared as they expected and the magazine had tried to make capital out of the school's being linked with Reid's supposed playboy reputation. But it went almost unnoticed in the avalanche of publicity surrounding his engagement to Penny.

Several publications would have pounced at the first hint of scandal but they had reprinted the photo with a new slant entirely, crediting Suzie as the force behind the romance.

Any ill effects from the original photo were more than offset by the excitement generated at the school for its role as Reid Branden's matchmaker. Without the engagement, things would have been very different, Reid was well aware.

It was difficult to think of himself as an engaged man. Penny certainly didn't act like a doting fiancée, except when they were in public together. Then he couldn't fault her performance, although anyone close enough to see her eyes might have had some doubts. She still looked at him as if she hated him, which was at odds with the way she reacted when he touched or kissed her.

Women were an enigma, he thought not for the first time. In his arms she practically melted, her heartbeat gathering so much speed he could feel it pounding against his chest.

He wasn't entirely immune, he had to admit. She turned him on in a way no other woman ever had, despite the misgivings he still held about her. Maybe he should just go ahead and marry her and sort the rest out later.

His fingers stilled on the keys of his clarinet, the scales he'd been running through fading into the still morning air. In common with most musicians he practised every day, rain, hail, shine or Christmas, and usually he did it with a concentration that was the envy of his colleagues. Now, however, the thought of Penny had introduced a discordant note.

Living at Kangaluma with her and young Suzie had shown him a glimpse of real family life. Getting up to the same faces each morning, having someone to enquire about his day when he got home at night, had a lot to recommend it.

Once, he'd imagined such a life with Penny, until she had shattered his trust in her. Was it too late to try again? They were spectacular together physically. Kissing her had reawakened some awfully pleasant memories on that score, and he'd resorted to enough cold showers lately to tell him there was still plenty there to be reckoned with.

But was it enough to build a future on?

Her stubbornness where the accident was concerned was still a bone of contention between them, as his casual probing had revealed. Unsettled by her conviction that there was more to the accident than she remembered, he'd searched through his insurance files to see if there was anything to back up her belief that she wasn't at fault. Not surprisingly, he'd found nothing new. Only the fact that she'd been drinking wasn't on record, thanks to his forbearance. She should be grateful instead of looking at him as if he had two heads.

Damn it, this was getting him nowhere. She wasn't going to change, so why was he wasting his time thinking about it? It was probably born of frustration, he told himself. Being engaged might be good for his image, but it was hell on his love-life.

Lifting his clarinet he began to play the Brahms Sonata in F minor. The difficulty of the piece demanded all of his concentration. And it was a lot more pleasant than a cold shower.

CHAPTER SIX

BEING engaged was playing havoc with her bank balance, Penny thought as she dressed for lunch with Reid. When his schedule allowed, he liked her to meet him at his office and join him for lunch at one of the many restaurants around the North Sydney area. It was purely to keep up appearances, she realised, but it meant dressing the part. Clothes which were fine for working from home were hardly suitable for dining in fashionable restaurants.

The mocha cotton-knit jacket and trousers she wore today were new, as were several outfits in her rapidly expanding wardrobe. She studied herself in the mirror, reluctantly admitting that it was an improvement. Her hair looked more stylish since she'd had the ends trimmed and flipped up with a few wispy curls softening her forehead.

She slipped a Nepalese medallion around her neck. The traditional symbol of harmony and balance was at odds with her confused state of mind. She didn't like being engaged to Reid. The papers made her sound like a piece of property he'd astutely acquired. Yet it wasn't wholly an endurance test either.

Suzie had assured her she looked 'cool'—her ultimate accolade, although her judgement was impaired by the pressure of a forthcoming exam. She was spending the night at a friend's house so they could study together. But her parting comment stayed with Penny. 'This marriage stuff must agree with you.'

Penny had dismissed the idea out of hand. 'You're imagining things.' Yet she couldn't argue with her reflection. She looked younger, more vibrant somehow, like Sleeping Beauty moments after the prince awakened her with a kiss.

Now who's imagining things? she asked herself. It must be the challenge of sparring with Reid on a daily basis which gave her such a glow.

It wasn't because she *enjoyed* having him under her roof. Yet there was a definite spark in the air when he was at home, which was simply missing at other times.

She was dangerously close to falling under his spell again, she realised. Having him live here, seeing him every morning and evening, was almost more than she could handle.

She knew she picked fights with him over the renovations purely as a defensive action and wondered if he knew it, too. His teasing responses to her attacks suggested as much.

Her breathing quickened as she remembered how he'd taken a stubborn jar from her hands and twisted it open effortlessly, handing it back with a wry look.

'I was managing just fine,' she insisted, but trembled as she realised it was no longer true. When he touched her, even for the most mundane reasons, and looked at her with such intensity, she wasn't fine at all. The opposite, in fact. She felt like a rag doll which was coming apart at the seams. 'I did manage before you moved in,' she insisted in a betrayingly defensive tone.

His hooded gaze mocked her. 'Ah, yes, all those live-in lovers.'

'At least they didn't tear my house apart so I can't even find a simple jar opener any more.'

'They probably didn't make your life half so exciting, either,' he denied, refusing to be drawn into another argument. He actually seemed to be enjoying this, she thought furiously. Couldn't he see what a strain it was for her, given how much they'd once shared?

That was then, this is now, she repeated like a litany. She swallowed the lump in her throat and picked up her handbag and car keys. Somehow she had to control these traitorous thoughts before they sent her crazy or before she revealed herself to Reid. She didn't know which would be the worst.

This time the parking attendant saluted deferentially as she occupied one of Reid's reserved parking spaces. It was amazing what an engagement-ring could do, she thought as she took the lift to the executive floor.

The ring had been another source of contention. The solitaire diamond was much too valuable for mere window-dressing, she had asserted. Inevitably, Reid's will had prevailed and she now wore the magnificent gem whenever she went out, although she still resolved to return it as soon as this farce was over.

She shuddered, thinking of the article which had appeared in *Inside* magazine a few days after Reid announced their engagement. The magazine had taken great delight in exploring every facet of Reid's love-life over the past few years, complete with photos, contrasting them with his recent involvement as Suzie's mentor. The intention was obviously to cast an unsavoury light on the whole mentor programme. It was so wrong and evil that she could hardly believe there wasn't some law to prevent it. Only Reid's quick thinking had prevented other publications from seizing on the idea. Now they were much too preoccupied with the more romantic story of the engagement.

Penny twisted the ring on her finger. The mentor programme meant so much to Suzie and to other talented youngsters. Penny's sacrifice was worth it for their sake. All she had to do was keep it in mind, however hard this became. It didn't help to realise how miserable the photos of Reid with other women could make her feel.

Tonia Rigg was in her office when Penny appeared. Since the announcement she had managed to occupy herself elsewhere during Penny's visits. The message wasn't lost on her.

The assistant inclined her head marginally. 'Reid's in conference,' she said flatly, her eyes indicating the door which Penny now knew led to his inner sanctum.

She would be pleasant if it killed her, Penny resolved. She nodded. 'He said his meeting might intrude on our lunch date but I don't mind waiting. He promised not to be long.'

'That's our Reid, a man of brief engagements,' Tonia emphasised the double meaning.

Five years ago Penny might have been intimidated by Tonia's supercilious attitude. Working overseas and fending for herself since her father's death had changed her. 'I take it you don't approve of our marriage plans,' she said bluntly.

'Since you ask, I don't approve of what you're telling the public, but I wouldn't go so far as to call them plans.'

Penny's breath caught in her throat. She hated confrontations and avoided them if at all possible but this one was long overdue. 'On what, precisely, do you base your presumption that our plans aren't bona fide?'

Icy green eyes impaled her. 'On the fact that Reid is still sleeping with me.'

A sharp pain twisted inside Penny but she resisted the sensation. She and Reid hadn't made any promises to each other beyond agreeing to a public engagement so she was surprised at the depth of feeling Tonia's statement aroused in her.

Then something flickered in the other woman's expression and Penny knew beyond doubt that she was lying. 'Really? I never credited you with imagination before, Tonia, but it requires ingenuity to invent such a fanciful idea.'

The whitening of Tonia's knuckles on the edge of her desk confirmed Penny's suspicion but Tonia's face remained as impassive as a china doll's. 'You seem sure it's all imagination. Am I also imagining the diamond-shaped birthmark on his hip?'

Shock made Penny feel ill and she swayed slightly, wishing she'd never started this. But it was too late now. 'I didn't say you've never slept with him,' she said, keeping her voice level with an effort. 'Only that you haven't done so since he proposed to me. Reid's a strong, virile man. We've been apart for five years. I doubt whether he spent them in a monastery.'

Saying what she knew to be true cost her more dearly than she expected, the words twisting inside her like knife-thrusts. She blamed the unpleasantness of this encounter. Just because she wore Reid's ring, she didn't care what he did or with whom, did she?

'All the same, he won't marry you. He's going to marry me,' Tonia insisted.

Penny's patience snapped. 'If he meant to marry you he would have proposed by now, so there's no point wasting your life waiting for something which isn't going to happen.' She leaned across Tonia's desk. 'We both know you sent that sleazy magazine photographer to my house, hoping the bad press would force Reid to leave, but it didn't work, did it? Of all people, you should know you can't force him to do anything. That includes putting a ring on my finger. It's there because he wants it there and it will stay for as long as he wants it to.' This last was the truth, at least.

Reaction made her tremble but she couldn't regret a word she'd said, although Tonia looked slightly stunned.

'So you worked it out,' she said with a taut smile. 'Pity, I thought it was bound to succeed.'

Having her suspicions confirmed was less satisfying than Penny had expected. She felt drained at the depth of the other woman's malevolence. She must have known her actions couldn't hurt Reid, so she had decided to strike at Penny through her niece.

Tonia obviously hadn't foreseen that Reid would solve the problem by proposing to Penny so her scheme had backfired royally. The thought gave Penny the strength to say, 'Now you know it didn't succeed, perhaps we can call off this ridiculous competition.'

With deliberate movements Tonia straightened the already pristine files on her desk. 'Ridiculous, is it? We'll see how ridiculous Reid thinks it is when he finds my resignation on his desk this afternoon, effective immediately, especially when I make it clear that you're responsible.'

What on earth had she provoked? 'Surely you don't need to resign?'

The other woman's mouth narrowed. 'Yes, I do. It's the perfect solution, in fact. Things are so hectic around here right now that I'd love to be a fly on the wall when you explain to Reid why I won't be around when he needs me.'

Penny had never intended this to happen and she was very much afraid that Tonia was correct in her assessment of Reid's reaction. 'What will you do if you leave here?' she asked.

'I'm not without resources. I'll manage to occupy myself until Reid contacts me. And make no mistake, he will. We go back a long way.' She walked out leaving Penny staring after her, badly shaken. Tonia couldn't be right, could she?

Reid's response was terrifying. 'You provoked her into what?' he echoed furiously when she told him what had happened.

Defensively she crossed her arms, disconcerted by his vehemence. Would he be this upset if the tables were turned and she, Penny, had walked out instead of Tonia? 'What was I supposed to do?' she demanded. 'Smile sweetly when she told me you're still sleeping with her?'

His sardonic gaze swept over her. 'What bothered you the most—Tonia's behaviour or the idea of me sleeping with her?'

She feigned indifference. 'Why should either option trouble me unduly?'

'You are supposed to be my fiancée.'

She swallowed hard, wishing she'd left the office door open when she joined him after his conference ended. The suite was enormous with two walls of glass overlooking Sydney Harbour but it managed to feel cramped with just the two of them in it. 'We both know this engagement is a useful fiction. It doesn't really mean anything.'

He rested one hip on the corner of his desk, folding his arms so he looked every inch the corporate giant with hardly a trace of the dedicated musician on view. 'I don't owe you any explanations for my actions but, if it helps, I haven't slept with Tonia since we made our announcement. Despite what you evidently think of me, I do have my own code of honour.'

Despite her brave assertion to Tonia, Penny hadn't been at all sure of her facts until now. A flood of quite unwarranted relief coursed through

PLAY

HARLEQUIN'S

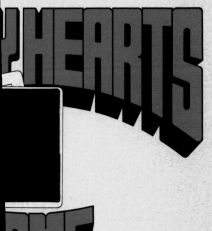

HEARTS

GAME

AND YOU GET

- FREE BOOKS
- FREE GIFT
- AND MUCH MORE

THE PAGE AND
YOURSELF IN

PLAY "LUCKY H
AND YOU GET . .

★ Exciting Harlequin Romance®

★ Plus a Lovely Simulated Pearl

THEN CONTINUE
LUCKY STREAK W
SWEETHEART OF

1. Play Lucky Hearts as instructed o

2. Send back this card and you'll rec
   Romance® novels. These books ha
   each, but they are yours to keep a

3. There's no catch. You're under n
   We charge nothing — ZERO —
   you don't have to make any mi
   purchases — not even one!

4. The fact is thousands of readers en
   from the Harlequin Reader Servi
   of home delivery. . .they like getti
   months before they're available in
   discount prices!

5. We hope that after receiving yo
   remain a subscriber. But the ch
   or cancel, anytime at all! So wh
   invitation, with no risk of any

NOT ACTUAL SIZE

This lovely necklace will add glamour to your most elegant outfit! Its cobra-link chain is a generous 18" long, and its lustrous simulated cultured pearl is mounted in an attractive pendant! Best of all, it's **absolutely free**, *just for accepting our no-risk offer!*

HARLEQUIN'S

With a coin — scratch off the silver card and check below to see what we have for you.

YES! I have scratched off the silver card. Please send me the free books and gift for which I qualify. I understand that I am under no obligation to purchase any books, as explained on the back and on the opposite page.

316 CIH AWF5 (C-H-R-06/95)

NAME

ADDRESS   APT.

CITY   PROVINCE   POSTAL CODE

Twenty-one gets you 4 free books, and a free simulated pearl drop necklace	**Twenty gets you 4 free books**	**Nineteen gets you 3 free books**	**Eighteen gets you 2 free books**

All orders subject to approval. Offer limited to one per household and not valid to current Harlequin Romance® subscribers.

© 1991 HARLEQUIN ENTERPRISES LIMITED.   **PRINTED IN U.S.A.**

THE HARLEQUIN READER SERVICE®: HERE'S HOW IT WORKS

Accepting free books places you under no obligation to buy anything. You may keep the books and gift and return the shipping statement marked "cancel". If you do not cancel, about a month later we'll send you 6 additional novels, and bill you just $2.74 each plus 25¢ delivery and GST*. That's the complete price—and compared to cover prices of $3.50 each—quite a bargain! You may cancel at any time, but if you choose to continue, every month we'll send you 6 more books, which you may either purchase at the discount price...or return at our expense and cancel your subscription.

*Terms and prices subject to change without notice.
Canadian residents will be charged applicable provincial taxes and GST.

CDMA
Member

0195619199-L2A5X3-BR01

HARLEQUIN READER SERVICE
PO BOX 609
FORT ERIE ON L2A 9Z9

MAIL▷POSTE
Canada Post Corporation/Société canadienne des postes

Postage paid   Port payé
if mailed in Canada   si posté au Canada

Business   Réponse
Reply   d'affaires

0195619199   01

If offer card is missing, write to: Harlequin Reader Service, P.O. Box 609, Fort Erie, Ontario L2A 5X3 her until she quelled it. She wasn't supposed to care what he did.

She took refuge in anger. 'Am I supposed to be flattered? I haven't slept with anyone else either, so we're even.'

His eyes narrowed and a dangerous gleam came into them. Purposefully he slid off the desk and loomed over her, placing his hands lightly on her shoulders. 'At last, a little honesty. You're annoyed because you feel I'm neglecting you.'

The heat of his touch radiated through her jacket, adding to her sense of outrage. 'You mean neglected as in sex-starved? You must be out of your mind.'

His heavy-lidded gaze lingered on her for what seemed like an eternity until he lifted a finger and lazily traced the outline of her mouth which was set in a determined moue. 'Not starved so much as deprived,' he murmured. 'Especially considering how things used to be between us.'

Her body insisted on remembering even as her mind recoiled from the seductive recollection. His closeness, the spicy aura of his aftershave lotion and an indefinable maleness enveloped her, threatening her senses with immediate overload.

Without conscious intention, she closed her eyes against the sensory onslaught and swayed towards him.

She held her breath as his lips brushed her hairline. Then with cruel suddenness he moved away. Instead of feeling relieved, she was frustrated to discover she felt like a child tantalised with a treat only to have it snatched away.

His obvious amusement deepened her sense of confusion. She was supposed to dislike him, so why did the very thought of his possession make her heart pound so hard it felt as if it was about to leap from her chest? 'You're wrong,' she denied bravely. 'I'd die before letting you make love to me.'

He tut-tutted reprovingly. 'Such an extreme re-action to an act of mutual seduction. For make no mistake, it would have been mutual, Penny. You deny it now, but a moment ago you were more than willing to rekindle some wonderful memories with me.'

Inwardly she was trembling with the forces he'd awakened in her, forces of such intensity that she could hardly believe it had taken no more than his touch to bring them to life. 'In your dreams,' she retorted, trying not to let him see how badly he'd affected her.

He was unperturbed. 'In my dreams and in yours. Haven't you lain awake at night thinking of what we once shared? Imagining how it was . . . and how it could be again?' He wasn't touching her and yet he was. Her skin burned wherever his gaze alighted, until his look might as well have been his hands, commanding her to respond to his touch as she'd done so readily five years ago.

'No, I haven't,' she lied. Admitting that she had, indeed, spent futile nights yearning for what they'd lost was tantamount to inviting a revival. While he still felt the same about her, a revival was out of the question.

'I could make you eat those words,' he said, challenge lighting his eyes. 'But I won't for now. I'd rather you retract them of your own accord.'

Why was he doing this? Surely keeping up appearances required only an outward show? There were still some places even the paparazzi didn't go. 'I wouldn't hold your breath,' she told him. 'You could have a long wait.'

A humourless smile lifted the corners of his mouth. 'We'll see. Perhaps lunch will improve your mood and make you more tractable.'

She shot him a killing look. 'Tractable as in docile and easily managed? It would take more than a lunch to pull that one off.'

His hand tightened on her elbow as he steered her towards the door. 'Another challenge, Penny? What's gotten into you today?'

She tried to tell herself her volatile mood had nothing to do with Tonia's scheme, or her claim to be intimately acquainted with a certain diamond-shaped birthmark on his hip.

Lunch was a tense affair which wasn't improved by the interested looks they attracted from the other diners. She should be used to Reid's celebrity by now but it still bothered her to be the focus of so many eyes.

'Ignore them. They'll soon tire of watching us eat,' he advised, sampling his grilled barramundi with obvious enjoyment.

She picked at her Caesar salad but could barely swallow a mouthful. 'Doesn't it bother you to be watched wherever you go?'

He shrugged. 'It doesn't bother me. The support
of those same people helped me get where I am
today.'

It was an attitude she hadn't considered. She tried
to follow his lead and ignore the stares. 'I really
am sorry about what happened with Tonia today.
I didn't mean to provoke her resignation.'

His eyebrow arched. 'We both know which road
is paved with good intentions. The fact remains that
it's happened at a highly inconvenient time for me.'

A host of possible reasons flashed through her
mind and she was foolishly glad of his assurance
that he wasn't involved with Tonia. This would have
to stop, she chided herself silently. There was no
need to play the role of jealous fiancée to extremes.

'The company is a major sponsor of the
Australian music industry awards,' he continued.
'Tonia was handling our involvement.'

'I didn't notice any staff shortages at North
Sydney,' she pointed out, rather more waspishly
than she had intended.

He gave her an assessing look which said he was
more aware of her thought processes than she
wanted him to be. 'Tonia's staff will fill the breach
at the corporate level but Tonia had other
responsibilities.'

To him, she couldn't help wondering despite his
assurance. 'Surely one of her assistants can fill in?'
she supplied, and was annoyed to find the prospect
equally dismaying. What on earth was going on
here?

He toyed with his wine glass, his intense scrutiny
fixed on her. 'There's another solution. Since you

created the problem, it's appropriate that you should take Tonia's place until the music awards are over.'

What did he have in mind? The possibilities rocked her until she realised he meant at the awards themselves. 'I couldn't,' she said, hating the very thought of such a public appearance at his side.

'You can and you will,' he said with deadly seriousness. 'Tonia was my right hand at industry functions. You've seen the media response to our engagement. Can you imagine the publicity if I arrived at the ceremony with a strange woman at my side?'

'It wouldn't occur to you to hire a right-hand *man*?' she threw at him, unprepared to admit how disturbed she was at the thought of another woman on his arm.

The faintest trace of amusement lightened his dark features. 'Attending the awards with a man would cause an even greater sensation.'

'You know it wasn't what I meant. Can't you hire a man for your office and... and attend the function alone?'

He leaned closer, resting his chin on one hand. To an observer, they might be exchanging intimacies but his words were pointed. 'The office isn't the problem. My staff can handle the administrative side. But the Press aside, we will need a chaperon for Suzie.'

Confusion coiled through her. 'What does Suzie have to do with this?'

'A feature of this year's awards is a series of performances by rising young stars. Suzie deserves the chance to be among them.'

Her mind reeled. Suzie would be playing for the cream of the music industry, her performance televised. Who knew what could come of it? 'You planned this as a way to get my co-operation, didn't you?' she asked suspiciously.

'I planned it because Suzie has a remarkable talent which deserves recognition.'

She was outmanoeuvred and he knew it. 'Very well, I'll play my part for Suzie's sake. But this has to end when my sister gets back and Suzie goes home. You can't ask more of me than that.'

His eyes flashed a challenge at her over his cupped hand. 'I can ask a great deal more of you, my dear Penny, but no more than I believe you're capable of giving.'

'As long as your demands stop at the office,' she said, feeling an unwelcome surge of excitement along her spine.

A sardonic lift of his eyebrows was her response. 'Considering that my office is equipped to function as a second home, I see no reason to regard that as a limitation.'

She swallowed hard. Remembering what they'd once shared was having a devastating effect on her equilibrium and she had a feeling that he knew it. He was playing her with all the skill of his beloved clarinet, and her breathing felt laboured as she monitored her chaotic responses. 'Will you stop this?' she hissed at him. 'I won't co-operate unless you promise to treat me with some respect.'

His hand slid across the table and his fingers closed over hers, his grip gentle but inexorable. 'Oh, but I will respect you, in the morning too, I assure you.'

'Why, you...' She tried to pull her hand free but his grip was like steel, his fingers strengthened by years of disciplined music practice. Without relaxing his grip he moved his thumb in a circular motion across the sensitive pulse-point at her wrist. In spite of her anger, heat flared from the spot all the way along her arm. She felt her face flood with colour.

Seeing the highly visible effect he was having, he gave a wintry smile. 'If you make this a contest of wills I guarantee you'll lose. Even as you tell yourself you hate me, you're imagining how it would feel if I touched your body like this instead of your wrist.'

It was so close to the truth that she began to tremble with betraying reaction. 'You're unbelievable. Why are you doing this to me?'

'Isn't it obvious? Being engaged to you has reawakened passions supposedly dead and buried—in both of us. You won't admit it because it would mean admitting that the years you spent running away from me were a mistake.'

To her horror, her vision blurred and she blinked hard. She would not give him the satisfaction of her tears. It would be almost like admitting he was right. 'There's more to a relationship than passion,' she told him unsteadily, although his touch was making it harder and harder to keep in mind.

'Who said I was referring only to a physical relationship?' He spoke so matter-of-factly that he could have been discussing business affairs. 'I was thinking of making our engagement a genuine one.'

Her mouth went dry and she wished she'd allowed him to order something stronger than Perrier water for her. 'You can't really want to marry me?'

'Is it so surprising? We came close to this point five years ago.'

And she remembered only too well what had happened. Never would she forget his disgust and horror after he lifted her clear of the wreckage. He'd looked as if it was an effort even to touch her. Afterwards, everything had been different.

He'd waited for her to admit that the accident was her fault. She had had too many drinks at the party then overruled Tonia's advice against driving back to the hotel. Admitting it would have healed things between them, because she knew it was her stubbornness more than the accident itself which infuriated him. So why did she find it so hard to do?

Because in her heart of hearts she didn't believe she was to blame, no matter how it looked to Reid. With no witnesses and the damning evidence of her presence behind the wheel when he found them, she had no way of proving her innocence. Nor could she remember anything clearly between leaving the party and recovering consciousness in Reid's arms. Yet somehow she knew there was more. If only she could dredge the truth out of her mind. But years of trying hadn't helped.

'Tell me one thing,' she said carefully, trying to suppress even the faintest twinges of hope. 'Do you still believe I crashed your car five years ago?'

His silence told her everything she needed to know.

'Nothing's changed, has it?' she asked dully.

His expression hardened. 'This is hardly the time and place to discuss it.'

'When will we discuss it—when we have our first argument and you remind me of how irresponsible I am, behaving with the same recklessness you remember so well?'

Thunder darkened his expression and his brows drew together in a disapproving line. She'd kept her voice low and he did the same, but his tone was still vibrantly angry. 'You're being ridiculous, worrying over something that would never happen.'

The blurring of her vision increased and she dashed a hand across her eyes. 'Am I? My father had one affair, just one indiscretion in all his years of marriage. My mother generously forgave him for it, then made sure he was never allowed to forget it. I don't want a marriage like that.'

'I see.' He signalled for their bill and dealt with it grimly, then eased her chair out. 'Let's go.'

'Where are we going?'

'Somewhere we can talk this out. There's something I want you to see.'

His hold on her elbow was punishing as he escorted her out to where a valet waited with his car. 'You're frightening me. What's this all about?' she asked as they pulled out into the traffic.

He spared her a black look. 'It's time you found out why I feel the way I do about drunk drivers. Maybe it won't change anything. Maybe you only want to see your own point of view. Either way, we'll understand each other a whole lot better.'

He drove in silence until they reached his office building where he took her, not to the executive floor but to the penthouse floor above, to a flat he informed her was provided for corporate visitors and his own use when he worked late into the night. 'This is the closest place I have to a home at present,' he told her as he showed her inside.

It was hardly homelike. She found the preponderance of chrome and black leather cold and unfriendly, although the view from the living areas was breathtaking. Ignoring her attempt at small talk he flipped switches on a hand control until a wall slid back to reveal state-of-the-art television and video equipment.

'Sit down,' he instructed.

Her stomach churned alarmingly, threatening to unburden itself of the expensive lunch they'd just consumed. 'I won't until you tell me what this is about.'

He continued sorting through video cassettes until he located the one he wanted. Slamming it into a machine, he crossed the room to her, the remote control in hand.

Before she could react he had wrapped an arm around her waist and carried her down with him on to the leather-covered sofa. Squirming and protesting were ineffectual. He simply pinned her against him, her struggles making no impact whatsoever.

'You brute, let me go,' she gasped, her breathing constrained by the tightness of his hold. His arm was a steel band around her shoulders, imprisoning her against his muscular body. Every lean contour was outlined against her. She had never been so aware of him as a man before, nor so alarmed by the ease with which he had overpowered her. The realisation provoked a confusing mixture of anger and unwelcome excitement.

He seemed unmoved by her confusion, fixing his gaze grimly on the huge television screen. With his free hand he thumbed the remote control and the set sprang to life. 'Now learn why I feel the way I do,' he grated.

In horrid fascination she watched, her struggles ceasing as she realised what she was being asked to watch.

It was newsreel footage from a car accident, roughly edited so it jumped from scene to scene. But there was no mistaking the content. Two cars were twisted into such surreal shapes it was hard to tell where one ended and the other began. There was no commentary, only the relentlessly graphic scenes of death and destruction.

She gave a gasp as the camera closed on the police rescue squad who were cutting bodies from the wreckage. 'This part was edited for television,' he informed her, his voice so cold that she recoiled inwardly. She wished it could be edited for her, too. The sight was almost more than she could bear.

Then the police were seen interviewing a man who was drunk and crying, either with shock or remorse she wasn't sure. It was clear he had been the driver of the car at fault, because he was soon led away to the police car, the tears still streaming down his face.

Her own face was wet, she realised when Reid snapped the television off. 'Dear heaven, what was that?'

'It was newsreel footage of the accident which killed my parents,' he informed her coldly. 'Years later I was setting up a television special and came across the film in a photo library. I kept it as a reminder of the evil that people can do.'

She turned blazing eyes on him. 'If you mean people like me, why don't you say so?'

His eyes were shining but beneath the betraying film was obsidian blackness. 'If the cap fits...'

Her hands clawed the air. 'How do I know whether the cap fits or not? You think I'm as pathetic as that drunk on the tape. Showing it to me only proves it. But I know it wasn't like that. I don't even know *how* I know. Sometimes I have dreams about the accident but it's gone when I wake up, so I can't prove that something's missing. I only know it is.'

A towering rage such as she had never seen before darkened his expression. His fingers flexed as if he would like to test them around her throat and she flinched inwardly but kept her back straight. 'By all that's holy, you're still clinging to the fantasy that it wasn't your fault. *That's* the real problem between us. But if you weren't driving, then who was? Tonia was unconscious in the passenger seat. There was no one else in the car.'

She had always suspected Tonia but couldn't dispute the facts. 'You checked to see she wasn't faking, I suppose?'

His disgusted look raked her. 'No eye movement, no response to stimulus usually adds up to unconsciousness, as I understand it.'

'Well maybe we had a driver who panicked and ran away after the crash.'

'And maybe the driver stayed and let her memory run away.'

She began to tear at the ring on her left hand, tears blinding her as the band refused to slide over her knuckle. 'I'm finished with this engagement. I hate you, do you hear, I hate you!'

She gasped as his fingers closed around her hand, staying her panicky movements. Slowly, inexorably, he brought her closer to him until their bodies were aligned. His heartbeat throbbed through her in time with her laboured breathing. Struggling was futile. He was much too strong. In any case, struggling seemed less and less important as other, more primitive instincts threatened to overwhelm her.

'That's better,' he said as her struggles subsided. 'It's time you learned that you can't solve anything by running away.'

CHAPTER SEVEN

TENSION vibrated through her as he raised her left hand slowly, deliberately to his mouth. Her finger was reddened from tugging at the ring and he pressed his lips to the mark, the tip of his tongue salving the tender flesh.

White heat flared through her. She tried to pull free but his grip tightened. His eyes challenged her to renew the struggle.

So he wanted a fight, did he? Deliberately she held herself quiescent, although a volcano of feelings surged close to the surface. She would not give him the satisfaction of struggling so he could conquer her.

But something was wrong. Muscles which should have been stone yielded to his touch as he stroked her shoulders and the slim column of her throat. She could barely restrain the moan which formed deep in her throat.

Cupping the sides of her head, he tilted her face upwards. Nervously she licked her lips and saw the muscles work in his jaw. Then he clamped his mouth over hers, driving every sensible thought out of her head.

She should hate him, hate what he was doing to her, but the taste of him ... the tantalising flicker of his tongue against her teeth was the stuff madness was made of. Her mind reeled and she clutched at him, unwillingly affected by the perception of muscles rippling under her hands, by hard flesh and sinew straining against impeccably tailored cloth. It was like feeling a surprise package with your hands, the suspense sweetly agonising, the possibilities infinite.

For fleeting moments she gave herself up to the exhilarating sensation, as he continued to kiss her with a thoroughness which left her breathless. A thousand 'if only's skated through her mind until she groped for some vestige of sanity. Given the way he felt about her, did she want to start this again?

Did she have a choice?

His fingers threaded through her hair, the gentle pressure making her scalp tingle. She parted her lips to protest and regretted it as he deepened the kiss, ecstasy spearing to the centre of her being.

She wasn't sure which of them she hated most at that moment—him for forcibly reminding her of the chemistry which still crackled between them, or herself for offering so little resistance. It was all she could do not to melt into his embrace and surrender to whatever demands he chose to make.

Where was her pride, her self-respect? How could she consider surrendering to a man who thought so little of her? Her palms beat at his shoulders. 'Let me go.'

His arms dropped to his sides but he stayed close, his cynical expression making her want to hit him. 'Still having a problem with honesty, Penny?'

She flinched but held her ground. 'No problem at all. Letting you touch me was the dishonest move, knowing what you think of me.'

'You're so sure you know what's in my mind,' he observed. 'I can assure you if you did you would be blushing to the roots of your beautiful bronze locks.'

His caressing look was all too revealing and she dropped silky lashes to hide the consternation he would almost certainly read in her eyes. 'I...I should go home,' she managed in a hoarse whisper.

'But you are home.' Before she realised what he meant to do, he had crossed to the front door. She heard an ominous click then he pocketed a key.

He had locked her in! The thoughts which ran rampant through her mind at the realisation astonished her. Where was the shock, the indignation? What flowed through her veins was much more primitive, almost unbearable in its honeyed sweetness, until she reminded herself that personal magnetism had been his hallmark as a performer. Critics had described him as being able to make a woman want him with a look. Aware as she was of his fatal charm, she'd be mad to let herself be manipulated by it.

'Open the door and let me out of here,' she insisted, hating the betraying huskiness which coloured her voice. 'What will people think?'

'They'll think we're fortunate to be so in love we can't wait for our wedding-night.'

So this was all about his image, lending weight to the fiction that they were engaged. An inexplicable sense of disappointment weighed her down, making her tone brittle. 'Should I check under the bed for paparazzi?'

His tongue clicked in disapproval. 'Cynicism doesn't become you, darling. This isn't for the public's benefit, it's strictly between you and me.'

'There is no you and me,' she protested weakly. 'Besides, I have to get home to Suzie.'

'No, you don't. She's at her friend's place, studying for a music exam. She told me so herself.'

She cursed Suzie's lack of guile. 'I'm not prepared for an overnight stay,' she tried again, the words almost stalling in her throat. It was true in every imaginable sense.

He gestured easily. 'This apartment caters for visiting executives. Most requirements have been provided for.'

Hot colour flooded her cheeks. 'I'm not wearing a nightgown provided for some businessman's bimbo.'

'Our visiting executives aren't exclusively male,' he reminded her, 'so your rather crude assumption is quite unwarranted.'

'Can you blame me for thinking it when you bring me here, lock me in and offer me borrowed finery? How am I to know it isn't a hobby of yours?'

'You know me better than that,' he said, clearly unimpressed by her outburst. 'I'd rather think of this as a night out of time, a chance to forget everything but each other.'

She swallowed convulsively, bewildered by her mixed reaction to the picture his words painted. Unwillingly she was carried back to when love had motivated his actions. How could she compare this travesty with the precious memories of that time? Yet the liquid velvet in his voice forced her to remember. Her knees began to buckle.

He was beside her in an instant, lifting her into his arms. 'I'll never forgive you for this,' she vowed as he carried her into the bedroom.

He lowered her on to the vast bed. The soft texture of the white faux fur spread brushed her skin, bombarding her mind with a dizzying array of sensations.

He leaned over to unbutton her jacket. She knew she should fight to escape this silken prison. But even with her eyes closed she was spellbound by his nearness, the musky male scent of him, his touch which seemed to be everywhere. Her mind was at war with her body.

It had been so long since she'd last been held like this, caressed like this, wanted like this. Was it so wrong to take something for herself out of it all? A night out of time, he had promised. Could she see it the same way, as a rare and precious experience which had no relevance to the rest of her existence?

No, came the denial inside her head. He could command her physically—was already doing so, if she was honest about it—but he had no right to demand her approval. He hadn't withdrawn his censure so he couldn't expect her willing participation.

She tried to struggle to her feet but was hampered by her undone clothing strewn around her.

'Let me up,' she insisted. 'This has gone far enough.'

His palm caressed her cheek. 'Oh, no, my dear Penny. It hasn't gone nearly far enough.'

She glared her fury at him. 'I'll hate you for this.'

'So you say, but your body tells me otherwise. By the time I'm through, you'll beg me to make love to you.'

'Never,' she vowed, but some inner part of her feared it was only too possible. She had already given him more of herself than she had believed she would ever do again. Was it such a giant step to letting him possess her entirely?

There was to be no *letting* about it, she soon found as he began a systematic assault on her senses such as she had never experienced before.

Letting implied permission. Dear heaven, what she found herself giving him was more like an invitation. She had never imagined she would do such a thing, yet she was powerless to stop it. Didn't know if she wanted to stop it. Didn't know anything any more.

She clamped her mouth shut against the moan which threatened to erupt from her throat and turned her head to one side, refusing to look at him. She refused to give him the satisfaction of hearing her beg, although it would have been the easiest thing in the world to do, the way she felt right now.

What he did next turned her eyes round as saucers. She felt as if she was about to explode. 'What was that?' she gasped, her panting breath almost robbing her of speech.

Wry amusement lit his eyes. 'It's called the Troubadour's Touch.'

'I don't care what it's called. Where did you learn to do that?'

'I read widely,' was his pleased response. 'I take it you liked it?'

She shook her head wildly. 'I did nothing of the sort.'

'Then you won't want me to do it again?'

'No—yes...oh, please...' She was begging after all and couldn't seem to stop herself. He had made her want him despite her misgivings. No matter how she tried to tell herself she hated how he was making her feel, the words slid out. 'Yes, damn you, yes.'

He undressed swiftly. 'That troubadour knew what he was doing,' he said as he came to her at last.

She tensed, hating to admit even to herself that she craved a repeat of the mysterious experience. What sort of woman did it make her, to be so responsive to such wantonness against her better judgement? She should have turned herself to stone, but, pity help her, she became mindless the second he touched her again. Avoiding his gaze, she turned her face away, lest he see the surrender in her eyes.

He clasped her chin and made her look at him. 'Glory in what you feel. It's God-given and right, understand?'

It was right as long as it was between two people who loved each other, she thought. Then it was the ultimate expression of their love. What was it between her and Reid?

She was terribly afraid she knew the answer. Was it love, at least on her side? Perhaps she had never really stopped loving him, in spite of everything.

She wanted to believe it was pure chemistry, and it probably was on Reid's part. But for her it was a poignant reminder of what could have been.

She gave a long, shuddering sigh as she tried to sort out how she felt. Happier than she had ever felt before, yes, but bewildered as well. Physical pleasure might be enough for him, but how could it be enough for her? She had probably made the biggest mistake of her life by allowing it to happen.

Allowing? The thought almost made her laugh aloud. She had practically invited him. She had no one to blame but herself.

She took refuge in flippancy. 'So this is how it feels to be held captive in a harem.'

He raised himself on one elbow, regarding her with wry cynicism. 'It can hardly be called a harem, since you are the only female in residence.'

'In captivity, don't you mean?'

'You should be grateful for your captivity, as you call it,' he said mildly. 'Look what you'd have missed if I had allowed you to run away.'

Her body ached and a warmth pervaded her which made her want to hide her face with embarrassment. Her wanton response to him hardly bore thinking about. She certainly didn't want him to remind her of it. 'You didn't have to lock me in to prove your point,' she denied.

He traced a spiral across her fiery skin, drawing a reluctant gasp of reaction. 'Are you quite sure I locked you in?'

She sat up, linking her arms around her bent knees. 'But I saw you lock the door.'

'You saw me pocket a key but you never thought to test the lock.'

'Why, you bastard. If I'd known...'

'But you didn't,' he said shortly. 'For perhaps the first time in your life, you weren't permitted to run away. Doesn't the outcome tell you something?'

She dropped her head on to her bent knees. 'It tells me never to trust a man like you.'

'Did I hurt you?'

Her voice was muffled. 'No.'

'Did I disappoint you?'

Oh, heavens, how could she assess it when the very opposite was true? 'No.'

He crooked a finger under her chin and lifted her head. 'Then you're angry because I made you feel something you don't want to feel. Why not, Penny? What scares you about honest-to-God emotions so you run away from them?'

She plucked at the faux fur cover. 'If you must know, my parents had a rotten relationship. On the surface it was all sweetness and light but underneath was a cauldron of hurts and resentments which kept getting brought up whenever they had a disagreement.'

'Yet they stayed together.'

'For all the good it did Jo and me. One or other of them was always threatening to leave. Sometimes I think it would have been easier if they had done instead of keeping us on tenterhooks wondering if they'd still be there when we woke up in the morning.'

He slid an arm around her shoulder. It was unexpectedly comforting. 'In some ways I know how you feel. After my parents were killed I felt abandoned. My grandmother tried to fill the gap but it wasn't the same. Luckily my music got me through it and kept me sane.'

'My sister, Jo, was my ally,' she admitted. 'Unfortunately she left home when I was twelve. She went to work in Andrew's real estate agency and ended up marrying him. I really missed her, especially when he moved his business to Adelaide after Suzie was born. Letters and phone calls aren't quite the same.'

'In spite of your childhood experiences, Jo was willing to take a chance on marriage,' he pointed out.

Jo had always been made of sterner stuff. 'She's eight years older than me. Maybe she coped better with the insecurity.'

'I wonder.' He began to massage her back with slow, persuasive movements which reduced her bones to liquid. Contrarily, she was glad he hadn't tried to dismiss her fears about marriage with trite reassurances. His touch was far more comforting.

Gradually she felt the tension which always accompanied thoughts of her parents' marriage ebbing out of her.

She was drowsy when the doorbell chimed. Reid glanced at his watch. 'That will be our dinner. I thought you'd prefer to have it sent in than go out somewhere.'

And he could keep a better eye on her, came the unwelcome thought. If they went out she might...run away? It was daunting to think he knew her better than she knew herself. Did she really make a habit of running away from life's challenges?

While he belted a silk robe around himself and went to answer the door she remained lost in thought. She had gone to London to escape Reid's censure after the accident. Working as a copywriter, she had progressed to handling her own accounts and was on the verge of becoming the agency's senior writer when her father's failing health had brought her back to Australia. Was it also an escape from more responsibility than she really wanted?

Damn Reid for planting such doubts. Everybody couldn't have his supreme confidence. Not confidence—presence, she amended. Nor his combustible talent which so mesmerized his audiences and facilitated his business successes.

Everybody couldn't be perfect like Reid Branden.

'You can come out now.'

She emerged having worked herself back into a self-righteous fury which wasn't helped by the sight of a hotel trolley set for two, complete with a single red rose in a crystal vase and candles in silver holders.

Before joining him she had wrapped a bath sheet around herself and his eyes glinted ferally as she stalked bare-legged towards the table. 'Pardon me if I don't dress for dinner.'

Her caustic comment drew the opposite reaction. He offered her his hand. 'Compared to a few moments ago, you're positively overdressed.'

'Don't remind me. I'm disgusted by this whole scenario,' she said with far more conviction than she felt.

He poured champagne into two flutes and offered her one. 'You have a unique way of showing disgust.'

She was tempted to refuse the wine. Drinking it implied approval of his scheme to keep her here, which was the last thing she felt. But her nostrils twitched as they were assailed by delicious scents from under the silver covers. She was hungry, she realised. Refusing to eat would hardly change what had happened.

He uncovered salvers crusted with ice on which lay succulent oysters garnished with grated egg and caviar. Instead of placing a plate in front of her, he lifted a spoonful to her mouth. 'Oysters Tzarina. They're a favourite of mine.'

She opened her mouth to protest but was thwarted when he pressed the spoon against her lips, forcing her to take a bite. She glared at him, refusing to admit that it was indeed delicious. Being spoon-fed made her feel unnervingly fragile and vulnerable.

Determinedly she began to feed herself. 'What would you have done if I'd screamed for the delivery person to fetch the police?' she asked, swallowing another succulent oyster.

'I'd have apologised for the loudness of the television in the bedroom,' he said mildly, then fixed her with a speculative look. 'But you didn't scream, did you?'

Why not? she couldn't help wondering. Come to think of it, why hadn't she tested the doorknob to see if it was really locked? She wasn't sure she wanted to know the answer.

The oysters were followed by a delicious lobster mornay with crisp green salads and crusty bread rolls. Dessert was a confection of black cherries marinated in Kirsch and crested with cream. By the time they reached the coffee stage, a sense of wellbeing pervaded her.

Her contentment must have shown on her face because he regarded her with wry satisfaction. 'Romance and fine food are remarkably curative.'

Annoyed with herself for sinking into a torpor when she should be planning her escape, she snapped back, 'They can hardly cure lack of consideration or trust.'

His dark gaze flashed a warning. 'I thought I was most considerate this afternoon.'

'I didn't mean that,' she rejoined, blushing scarlet at the reminder. 'I was referring to the way you contrived to get me here, then refused to let me leave. You're right, I would have run away given half a chance.'

His throaty laughter mocked her. 'Liar. You had much more than half a chance to leave. I even promised not to make love to you until you begged me to. You can hardly call that coercion.'

Knowing he was right only fuelled her self-censure. 'All the same, it wasn't gentlemanly to use your greater *experience*——' she gave the word deliberate emphasis '—to manipulate me as you did.'

He lifted a cynical eyebrow. 'You seemed awfully open to manipulation.'

'I hated it, every minute of it.'

'Indeed?'

Before she knew what was happening he had skirted the trolley and lifted her bodily out of the chair. Her napkin fluttered to the floor and it was only by clutching at the towel that she prevented it from following suit. 'What do you think you're doing?'

'A little more manipulation,' he informed her, 'since it seems to be the best way I have of reaching you.'

She beat futilely at his shoulders and kicked her legs but might as well not have bothered. 'Control is all you understand, isn't it?' she fired at him, trying to ignore the way her traitorous body insisted on responding to him. She didn't want him to make love to her again, did she? Hadn't she learned anything from the past five years?

It seemed not, because part of her insisted on remembering when he had touched her with such love, such devotion that her eyes filmed as she brought it to mind.

His fingers grazed the wetness on her cheek. 'Tears, Penny?'

'I just want you to put me down,' she managed with an effort.

They had reached the bedroom and he obliged, the sight of the rumpled bed adding to her confusion as he lowered her onto it. 'Delighted to comply,' he said. 'Is there anything else you'd like me to do for you?'

Yes, like me, not just love me, her inner voice implored. Look at me the way you used to, with warmth and tenderness.

He *was* looking at her that way, she discovered with amazement when she opened her eyes. She tried to tell herself it was born of her own wishful thinking. It would vanish in the cold light of day, just as all the tenderness had vanished before. Still, it was tempting to believe it was real. As if in a dream she linked her arms around his neck and drew his head down to her. At his touch, her senses spiralled into overdrive.

This was how it should be, she thought as she felt herself cradled in strong arms. For fleeting moments she allowed herself to hope that there might be a chance for them after all.

He seemed to sense the change in her and surprised her by sliding her feet to the floor, although his palm rested maddeningly on her stomach.

'What is it?' she asked as uncertainty came flooding back.

'This seems to be the only place where we truly connect,' he said, beginning a nerve-shattering circular motion with his hand which made her back arch involuntarily, proving his point.

'I didn't think you cared about connecting,' she ground out, appalled by how easily he could make her forget all the reasons why this was madness.

He gave her an assessing look. 'I care about it a lot more than you realise. You see, I don't believe that you dislike me as much as you'd have me think. I've no doubt I remind you of an experience you'd rather forget, but it hardly makes me the ogre.'

It was hard to think coherently when he was touching her like this but she forced herself to concentrate. 'So it comes back to being my fault again.'

'Your words, not mine.'

She shook her head wildly. 'But it is what you think.'

'Is it so surprising after you took yourself off to London rather than face me?'

You could have come after me, she thought in silent anguish. She'd left a paper trail anyone could have followed, but he hadn't. She was forced to conclude that she had so disappointed him that he was finished with her for good.

'Let me go,' she pleaded. She must be mad, letting him make love to her when it couldn't change what had happened or how he felt about it, how he would always feel because of his parents. No matter how compatible they were physically, sooner or later her near-fatal error would cast a shadow over any happiness they managed to attain. Her parents' experience proved how inevitable it was.

'Now or in the morning?' he queried silkily.

Indecision gripped her. She had only to ask and he would release her. Why didn't she? Because she wasn't sure she wanted to. Tonight he had revived such wonderful memories that she wanted to hold on to them for just a little longer. Was it so wrong? 'In the morning, please,' she whispered, wondering what she had invited.

He stretched out beside her. 'You see? We do communicate better here than anywhere else.'

'It won't change anything,' she said, wondering if it was another brave fiction.

'Of course not.' He rained kisses across her eyelids while his hands explored the rest of her until a slow burn started deep inside her, threatening to consume her utterly.

Then to her frustration he pulled the fur covering over them both and rolled on to his side, his hand remaining on the curve of her breast.

He was going to sleep. She should have been relieved but felt contrarily disappointed. Of all the times to take her at her word, why did he have to choose now?

CHAPTER EIGHT

IT WAS raining, the hard, pitiless drops splattering against the windscreen like suicidal insects. The street-lights blurred into ribbons of shimmering light, creating a surreal landscape where dark figures moved and her heartbeats kept time with the throb of the windscreen wipers.

Suddenly a great mouth yawned out of the darkness ahead, its teeth glinting wickedly. No, not teeth. The front grille of an enormous truck. A scream lodged in her throat as the teeth swung away, missing them by inches. Horns blared a protest.

A high-pitched squeal of brakes took up the chorus and she hung on grimly as she slewed sideways, tossed around like a cork on an ocean, her seatbelt biting into her breasts. Then there was nowhere to go. A brick wall rose in front of them like the hand of a traffic policeman with graffiti painted incongruously across his giant palm.

Moments later the palm closed over her with a sickening crunch of metal and the world turned upside down.

'No!'

She awoke to the croaking sound of her own voice which still echoed in her mind as a full-throated scream. She looked around in a daze. Where was she?

Then she remembered. She had spent the night in Reid's company flat. The space beside her was empty but the pillow bore the imprint of his head. They had made love several times during the night, she recalled with a flush of mortification.

She was thankful he couldn't see the self-condemnation in her eyes as she heard him talking on the phone in the other room. Some kind of business discussion was involved, she gathered.

Her face was damp with perspiration and she trembled with the after-effects of the dream. Disturbed, she drew her legs up and pulled the soft fur cover around her shoulders but the warmth was slow to seep into her body. Why had she dreamed of the accident now?

It was Reid's tape, she reasoned, her heart aching for him as she remembered his face as he watched. No wonder his disapproval of her was so strong, except for one area where she evidently satisfied him. Thinking of how much made her want to bury her head under the covers in embarrassment.

She tried to remember the dream. Everything had seemed clearer then. Swerving to avoid the big truck, hitting the brick wall. It was all vivid except for one persistent problem. In the dreams she was never behind the wheel.

She couldn't be sure the truck had actually existed or if her imagination had supplied it as a face-saving explanation for the crash. Bumping her head had erased her memory, except for the tantalising glimpses she saw in the dream but they faded as soon as she awoke.

She gave a sigh. Going over it in her mind wouldn't help. Nor would it bring Reid into the bedroom to enfold her in strong arms and tell her everything was fine. Making love to her was one thing, but loving her was another altogether. It was as much a fantasy born of her own needs as her dream of viewing the accident from the passenger side of the car.

Reid was still tied up with his conference call, pacing the floor and gesturing to an unseen party on the other end of the line, so she slipped into the adjoining bathroom and showered quickly and quietly. The flat was as well equipped as he'd promised and she'd emerged feeling more like her usual self, except for an assortment of aches in unaccustomed places which made her blush when she noticed them.

Her suit was uncrushable and looked reasonably fresh when she put it on, although she was aware of the talk it would cause if she was seen leaving in the same outfit in which she had arrived yesterday. Well, let them talk. She found she no longer cared very much what anyone else thought.

Was Reid having an effect on her personality as well as everything else in her life? Even a week ago it would have seemed unthinkable. Now she was forced to think it. The changes in her couldn't be ignored any more than she could ignore the disturbing physical evidence of his attentions which her shower revealed.

Reid had finished his call when she emerged. His eyes lingered on her for long minutes. What did one say to a man after a night such as they had spent together? Did she thank him or accuse him? She felt like doing both and neither. It was an effort to meet his eyes.

He had no such qualms. 'You look lovely this morning, Penny. Come and join me for breakfast.'

Last night's trolley had been replaced by a fresh setting for two, this time with breakfast delicacies like fresh fruit and pastries whose fragrance made her mouth water.

'I don't feel lovely,' she denied in a low voice. 'My clothes are crumpled, my hair's a mess. Goodness only knows what I must look like.'

'You look like a woman who has been well and truly loved. Your mouth has a delectable fullness which only comes from being thoroughly kissed and your eyes have a sparkle which tempts me to abandon all my plans for the day and remain here with the door locked.'

The reminder of how he had tricked her into staying gave her the strength to ignore the flames his suggestion ignited inside her. 'Should I be flattered at the idea of being used as some sort of plaything?' she challenged.

His eyes narrowed, the pupils piercingly brilliant under the lowered lashes. 'There was no using about it. I gave you every bit as much pleasure as I took.'

For want of something to do she took a seat facing him across the trolley but kept her head lowered. 'I can hardly deny it, can I?' Had he any idea how much the admission cost her?

'Well, well. Honesty at last. We *are* making progress.'

Her head came up and she fixed him with a mal-
evolent stare. 'No, we're not. This ends here and
now.' She waved away the coffee he held out to her.
'I don't want anything other than to be allowed to
go home.'

He set the cup down and tossed a crumpled
napkin onto the table. 'I'll drive you to Kangaluma
myself.'

'Don't bother. My car's downstairs.'

He swore loudly. 'So we're back to this again.
It's easier to run away than admit that something
extraordinary happened between us last night.'

'We had sex,' she said dully.

'No, we didn't. We made love, glorious,
passionate, set-the-night-on-fire love. There's a
difference.'

'Only in degree,' she insisted stubbornly. Love
didn't begin to describe what they had shared.

'Which afforded you no pleasure whatsoever?'
The question was cynically mocking.

'I've already admitted it did,' she cried on a de-
spairing note. 'What more do you want me to say?
That you're the world's greatest lover? Unlike you,
I'm in no position to judge.'

Had she really said such an awful thing? 'I'm
sorry, I had no right to suggest...'

'That you're the latest in a long line of women
I've pleasured?' His whiplash tone made her flinch.
'No, you have no right to make such an
assumption.'

All the same he didn't deny it, she noticed. She
remembered Tonia's avowed certainty that he would
contact her. To Penny's acute discomfiture she

found she cared very much about that. Yet she had no right to care. It was all too confusing and she ducked her head to conceal the betraying moisture which filmed her eyes.

'You have my apology,' she repeated.

'But nothing beyond it?'

What did he want from her? 'Isn't an apology enough?' she demanded hotly, as annoyed by her errant thoughts as his insistence that she admit to enjoying his lovemaking. Couldn't he see how conflicted she was? Part of her gloried in what he had made her feel and another part recoiled from the emptiness it highlighted in their relationship.

Panther-like, he moved around the trolley. 'Where you're concerned, it will never be enough.' His hand moved across the sensitive nape of her neck.

It was impossible to control the flush which sprang to her cheeks as her heart began a frenetic tattoo. 'Don't... Stop,' was all she could manage to say.

'Don't stop?' he drawled. 'I've hardly begun.'

Sweeping her hair aside, he bent his head and trailed feather-light kisses along her nape, while her heart thudded and her palms grew moist. When he tilted her head back and claimed her mouth as she had known he would, her eyes were shining.

Almost of their own accord her hands went up to cup his face. He deepened the kiss and she gave vent to a yearning sigh as all the reasons why this was wrong were submerged by the desire which flamed instantly to life.

For a few seconds temptation warred with common sense. Surrendering to the powerful currents swirling and eddying through her seemed far more appealing than fighting him. Was this what it was like to let yourself drown?

Barely aware of her actions she let him urge her to her feet. But when he moved towards the bedroom she came to her senses and hit out at the curve of his encircling arm. 'Why are you doing this?'

A raised eyebrow was his response. 'Need you ask? I want you, and your response tells me the feeling is entirely mutual.'

'You're wrong,' she denied, the lie filling her with despair. 'You don't even like me, but it's nothing compared to the way I feel about you.'

'You hate me?' he confirmed, sounding more amused than disturbed.

'Isn't it obvious?'

'What's obvious is that you hate the way I make you feel. But you didn't always. I remember nights when we barely slept, so anxious were we not to waste a moment when we could be scaling the heights together.'

She clamped her hands over her ears. 'Everything's changed since then. I've changed.' She didn't want to be reminded of what she'd lost. The last five years had been penance enough, seeing his image everywhere and knowing he was lost to her.

That was when she had decided to seek work overseas. Even then she couldn't leave without letting him know. But Tonia had called first to let her know that Reid would be changing advertising agencies. She hadn't believed the other woman until the move was confirmed in the trade press. Then it had really hit home to her that it was over. She had left for London without trying to see him again. Last night was more than she had bargained for, much, much more.

His hand grazed the side of her face, sending a shiver coursing down her spine. 'Some things haven't changed, such as your ability to drive me beyond sensible limits.'

She was perversely pleased by the discovery until she reminded herself that the limits were purely physical. 'Don't, please,' she said on a beseeching note. 'I can't go on being engaged to you under these conditions.'

A dangerous gleam brightened his eyes. 'Name your conditions. I may well choose to meet them.'

What would he say if she named unconditional love as her main requirement? She could well imagine the derision which would greet such an unreasonable expectation.

'I mean I can't go on pretending under any conditions,' she amended. 'The need for this charade has surely passed. The media have lost interest in the story about you and the school. The mentor programme is safe.'

'You're overlooking the tenacity of the Press. A suspiciously short engagement could send them digging around for reasons.'

'How much longer, then?'

'Is it such an endurance test? You didn't think so last night.'

She turned away, her face flaming. 'Must you remind me?'

'Must you fight me at every turn?'

Yes, if it was the only way to remain aloof from him when every instinct she possessed counselled surrender. For one insane moment she envied Tonia all those years of working alongside Reid, being his right hand—his lover? She had an almost irresistible urge to lead him back to the bedroom and make him forget that any other woman existed.

Trembling on the brink of submission, she pulled herself back barely in time. 'Take me home, please,' she whispered.

What was the matter with him? Reid thought furiously as he settled into the flow of traffic along Military Road. Penny had finally agreed to let him drive her home with the promise that he would have her car returned later in the day.

This hadn't turned out at all the way he'd planned. Keeping her away from the house overnight had been the only way he could spring his surprise. He hadn't intended to come on like the Sheikh to her. All that stuff about locking the door—where had that idea come from?

He certainly hadn't intended to show her the tape until his temper had got the better of him. If only she'd abandon her obsessive belief that she wasn't driving on the night of the accident, he wouldn't have put her through such an ordeal. Or himself for that matter.

Seeing the footage again had left him feeling raw inside, as if someone had stripped his nerve-endings as bare as electrical wiring.

He wasn't even sure why he'd kept the film at all. Maybe because it was his last contact with his parents and a reminder of how senselessly life could be snatched away.

Seeing it again had reminded him of the rage which had erupted inside him the first time, a killing rage. With no one to kill he had killed the world instead, first on the concert stage, then in the recording studio, and finally in the corporate world. Now he was ready for new challenges.

A home of his own fitted the bill. Kangaluma, he thought with a feeling of anticipation. Never had he wanted a property more.

He glanced at Penny, a study in vulnerability as she slumped beside him, her face turned towards the ocean-fringed parkland on their right. She certainly hadn't looked vulnerable last night. His hellicat, he thought, feeling the scratches she'd inflicted on his back at the height of their passion.

What would she say if he showed them to her? She'd probably turn a deep shade of scarlet. He was fairly sure she had no idea of the damage she'd inflicted.

And not only to his hide, he thought wryly. Pricing the renovations out of her reach so she would have to sell Kangaluma to him had seemed fairly logical at first. He had even convinced himself he was doing her a favour. When had he begun to have second thoughts?

'Were you expecting a visitor?' he asked as he rolled the big Mercedes in behind the builder's battered truck. A silver-grey Magna was parked alongside it.

'I wasn't but... that looks like Jo's car.' She bit her lip. 'She and Andrew aren't due back from Asia for weeks.'

'Maybe she tired of travelling and decided to come home early,' he speculated.

'It looks like it. I hope she hasn't been waiting for too long.' The idea of Jo knowing where she'd spent the night and with whom made her feel as uncomfortable, as if she was still accountable to her older sister. It was a foolish feeling but hard to shake off.

'Does she have a key?' Reid asked.

'She half-owns the place, remember? I'd better go inside and see what the problem is.'

He touched her arm. 'It might not be a problem.'

She gave him a dubious look. 'You don't know my sister. It takes something earthshaking to get her to change her plans.'

'I'll have a word to the builder and give you some time alone with her,' he offered, opening the passenger door for her.

His thoughtfulness drew a smile of appreciation. 'Thanks. You're right, it's probably nothing.'

But it wasn't nothing, she realised as she caught sight of Jo's upset expression. Her sister was in the kitchen making coffee when Penny walked in. 'Where on earth have you been? I was worried sick.'

Reminding herself that Jo was only concerned for her wellbeing helped Penny to hold back the reminder that she was twenty-six, not sixteen any more. Ever since their mother's death Jo had assumed a maternal role and Penny supposed it was hard to give up. 'I was out last night.'

'All night? Oh, Pen, I hope you were careful.'

To fend off what sounded like a potential lecture, Penny changed the subject. 'What time did you get in?'

'Just after seven this morning. Luckily I had my key with me. I hope you don't mind me letting myself in.'

'Of course not. This is your home, too.' Penny accepted the coffee her sister handed her, wrapping both hands around its warmth. 'Is something wrong?'

'Why should something be wrong?'

'You're home early. It isn't like you to change your plans without good reason.' She gave a nervous laugh. 'When we were kids, Dad always said he could set his clock by your schedule.'

With a wry grin, Jo sat down at the kitchen table and reached for her handbag. Pulling out a crumpled magazine cutting, she offered it to Penny. 'I came because of this.'

'Oh, no.' It was the story from *Inside* magazine with its photo of Reid and Suzie and the pathetic attempt to drum up a scandal by connecting his playboy image to the school's mentor programme. It had never occurred to Penny that copies might find their way to Asia and that her sister might eventually see one.

'Oh, yes. I know what this rag is capable of, but it didn't cushion the shock at seeing my own daughter in the middle of a story like this. What's going on, Pen?'

Penny felt for her sister, understanding her shock which must have been doubled by being so far from home.

'It's nothing like how they make it look,' she reassured Jo. 'Reid is involved with the mentor programme and he is helping Suzie with her music, but that's all there is to it, honestly.'

'I'll vouch for that,' drawled a baritone voice, and Reid stepped into the kitchen.

His arrival startled Jo into silence. 'You must be Penny's sister, Joanne. Reid Branden,' he said, offering her his hand.

'Mr Branden,' Jo's voice came out as a slight squeak. Penny had never seen her older sister so stunned before and she couldn't restrain a momentary thrill of pride. For a heartbeat she wished she were really engaged to him, if only for the effect he had on other women, her sister included.

In his impeccably tailored business suit he looked the image of prosperity and sophistication. Jo must be wishing she hadn't sounded so suspicious when she showed Penny the clipping. He was bound to have overheard.

If he had he gave no sign, although when he turned briefly to Penny, his right eye closed fractionally in what she could have sworn was a wink. She must be imagining things.

'You've done a remarkable job of raising Suzie,' he told Jo. 'Penny tells me you encouraged her to participate in the school's mentor programme, which is where I came in.'

Jo gulped. 'You're her mentor? She didn't tell me who she had in mind.'

'She probably thought I'd turn her down and didn't want to disappoint you. But her letter was so charming that I couldn't refuse. When I found out who her aunt was...' He let the sentence trail away, his gaze warming as he turned it on Penny.

Jo looked faint. 'You mean you and Pen are...the two of you...'

'Precisely.' He took pity on her. 'I understand you were living interstate but I'm sure you knew your sister and I were seeing each other before we went overseas.'

'Well, yes, but I didn't realise you were back together.'

'Neither did we until we met again to discuss Suzie's music. That photo was taken on the day we decided to announce our engagement. If the photographer had waited five more seconds, he'd have captured Penny bringing out the champagne to celebrate, with soda for your daughter, naturally.'

'Naturally. I don't know what to...of course I'm thrilled for you both. You know I want the best for you, Penny.'

'I know.' And Penny did. Jo might overdo the big-sister concern sometimes but she invariably had Penny's best interests at heart. She had been nothing but encouraging throughout Penny's previous involvement with Reid and she had nobly avoided any hint of lecturing after the break-up. Penny had never felt closer to her sister than at that time.

Now a glow of satisfaction warmed Penny's heart even though it was undeserved. She found she liked the thought of Jo being proud of her and it was obvious that Reid had charmed her utterly. She would have a lot of explaining to do when this was over but, for now, it felt good to be the object of her sister's obvious approval.

Recovering fast, Jo gestured towards the clipping. 'I'm sorry for over-reacting. When you're a mother yourself, Pen, you'll understand. All I wanted was to protect Suzie.'

'She was never in any moral danger, except in the minds of the gutter Press. I trust we've satisfied your concerns on that score?'

Jo's colour heightened. 'Of course, Reid, and thank you for helping her. It will mean so much to her.' She leaned forward. 'If you want the truth, I was ready to come home anyway. I find Asia so crowded and noisy, although Andrew loves the cut and thrust of being there. He stayed on while I came home.'

Reid put an arm around Penny's shoulders. It was all she could do to remain outwardly relaxed. 'We understand, don't we, darling? Your return is well timed to help Penny plan the wedding. Since you have no parents, I'll take care of everything, of course, but I bow to your expertise when it comes to the arrangements.'

Jo positively preened while Penny began a slow burn inside. How dared he involve her sister in plans he knew would never reach fruition? 'It's too early to discuss it yet,' she said through set teeth. 'Jo's feet have barely touched the ground.'

Her sister yawned delicately. 'You're right, I'm afraid. I'm going home to flake out, but later I'd love to see what you've been doing to the old place. It looks as if it's getting a new lease of life.' She smiled at Penny. 'And the house is not the only one.'

Sensing Penny's discomfort with this line of discussion, Reid stepped in smoothly. 'Actually the renovations are my doing. I've been using the house as my base so it seemed logical to put it in order.'

Jo refused to be sidetracked. 'And Penny's new glow—is that your doing too?'

His hand slid into Penny's. 'I would hope so.'

Jo looked satisfied. 'About time, too. Well, I'd better be off. I'll collect Suzie from school and we'll fetch her things tomorrow. I can't wait to see her again.'

Promising to call later when she was over her jet lag, Jo left at last. Her car door had barely slammed when Penny rounded on Reid.

'How could you?'

'How could I what?'

'Talk about a wedding which will never take place.'

'You could have told her the truth yourself,' he pointed out, his calmness infuriating.

Why hadn't she? 'If I had, she might have doubted my word about the story, too,' she defended herself.

He nodded tautly. 'Exactly. Now if you've finished arguing in circles, I have something to show you.'

He led her through the hall, which was emerging as a beautiful sanctuary now that the carved timber panelling had been replaced. The leadlight doors to the dining-room were closed and he opened them with a flourish. Something like triumph glittered in his dark gaze as he snapped on the light in the room.

'Oh, my lord.'

The room was finished down to a rich dark green paintwork highlighted by hand-made grape friezes. The colours were repeated in the detailing of the joinery, period fireplace and chandelier which were newly installed.

It was the painting which rivetted her attention. Since she'd been unable to get into the room while the tradesmen were there, it was her first sight of it in days. It had been cleaned and restored to astonishing brilliance. The crayon and distemper work might have been newly painted, so vivid was the sight of the Sirius, large enough for all her gear to be visible, riding out a mighty gale.

Penny had lived with the painting all her life and never before seen it in such splendour. Emotion threatened to choke her. 'How did you do it?'

'I've had the conservators working for days under cover of the other renovations.' He sounded satisfied, as well he might. With one act he had destroyed any chance she might have had of remaining mistress of Kangaluma.

Her body shook as she faced Reid. 'You planned this, didn't you? A night out of time, you called last night. It was more like out of harm's way while you laid claim to my home, wasn't it?'

'You're being ridiculous.'

'Am I? Then tell me you'll happily walk away from Kangaluma when this is over.'

Something unfathomable snapped in his eyes then was gone. 'I've made no secret of wanting either the house or its mistress.'

'No.' She shook her head as tears blinded her. He was quite amenable to a package deal if that was what it took to secure the house. But it wasn't enough for her.

Now she had the impossible burden of trying to repay him for the fortune he had spent.

It was so unfair that she wanted to weep, but she kept her shoulders back and her head high. 'Neither of us is for sale. With Suzie going home, there's no reason to continue this farce of an engagement so we may as well end it now. I'll find a way to pay you back for the renovations, I promise.'

He caught her shaking body to him. In spite of herself her senses leapt until she schooled herself to impassivity. 'There's only one form of payment I'll accept and that's your continued co-operation,' he ground out.

She had a choice between losing her home and her self-respect. 'You can't ask this of me.'

'I am asking it.' His thumb grazed the pulse point at her throat, gauging its hectic beating with satisfaction. 'So outwardly defiant, so inwardly passionate. You're a curious mixture, my little hellcat.'

'I'm not your anything. Let me go, damn you.'

'Not until you agree to appear as my fiancée at the music industry awards in a week's time. Exactly a week after that I shall sign over my interest in Kangaluma to you.'

Two weeks. Surely she could endure another two weeks of this if she had to? He was probably right about the danger of appearing to break it off too soon. And there was Suzie to consider. She was beside herself with excitement at the prospect of performing. 'Very well, I agree,' she conceded.

'A wise decision.'

It seemed ages before he put her away from him. Stumbling a little, she escaped to the kitchen, aware of an inner struggle which defied all reason. She had actually found herself wanting to agree to his terms when she should have fought him tooth and nail. Fighting him was becoming increasingly difficult, she acknowledged. He had called her compliance a wise decision, but it felt like the worst mistake of her life.

CHAPTER NINE

As THE night of the music industry awards approached, Penny's apprehension grew. It was one thing to attend such functions as part of a crowd, well out of the spotlight. But it was quite another to arrive on Reid's arm, knowing they'd be the focus of all eyes.

'I don't have anything suitable to wear,' she told him, taking refuge in the oldest excuse known to womankind.

His dark eyes bored into her. 'Is that the only obstacle to your enjoyment of the evening?'

'What else could there be?' Except Reid himself, of course. He had already informed her that the event would probably continue into the early hours of the morning so they would stay overnight at the hotel hosting the awards. She cherished not the faintest hope that he had reserved separate rooms for them and told herself it didn't bother her.

Not much it didn't.

He scribbled something on a card and handed it to her. 'Aloys is a friend of mine from the States. He should be able to help you.'

Her eyes widened. His friend was a famous American fashion designer who was currently in Sydney to assist a well-known charity. He had brought a small, terribly exclusive collection with him. 'I can't afford his prices.'

146

From his wallet he removed a platinum American Express card and handed it to her. 'Consider it an investment on my part.'

Fury boiled up inside her. 'Like the one you're making at Kangaluma? What are you hoping to do, buy me as well as my house?'

A momentary bitterness tightened his mouth. 'It can hardly be said to have worked at Kangaluma.'

'True.' In less than two weeks he would sign over his interest in the property to her and their arrangement would be at an end. The idea was less satisfying than she expected.

She picked up the card. 'As long as you don't mind throwing good money away, who am I to argue? At least you won't have to be ashamed of me on the night.'

Anger dilated his eyes and his hands flexed into fists before he relaxed them again. 'What makes you think I'd be ashamed of you, with or without designer finery?'

He couldn't actually be *proud* to have her on his arm? He didn't care enough for that. He must resent her challenging his good taste. 'It was only a thought,' she tried to make light of it.

'A thought you'd do well to forget,' he advised her.

Resentment surged through her. 'Otherwise you'll do what? Beat me?'

His eyes flashed a warning. 'Aren't you afraid of giving me ideas?'

She ignored the rush of warmth which infused her. 'You have more than enough of your own.'

'My creativity didn't seem to bother you a few nights ago,' he reminded her.

Something indefinable in his look made her catch her breath. She'd relived the events of that night more times than she wanted to admit. No matter how she tried, she couldn't recast herself as an unwilling participant and the thought mortified her.

He knew, she saw in his face. Resentment gripped her. 'It would have bothered me more if I'd known it was a scheme to keep me away from Kangaluma while you cemented your hold on it.'

He frowned ominously. 'My interpretation of that night evidently differs from yours.'

'And your interpretation is the right one, of course?'

'Not always. But I am right about one thing.'

She hardly dared voice the question. 'What?'

'In similar circumstances you'd respond exactly as you did before.'

He couldn't be right, yet she couldn't force out the denial he deserved. Perhaps because she couldn't bring herself to lie outright even to him. 'You'll die wondering,' she dissembled, 'because I'm going shopping.'

As she flounced out she was sure she heard the vibrato sound of his laughter. That was going to cost him plenty, she resolved.

The designer, Aloys Gada, was holding court from the presidential suite of his harbourfront hotel. Reid's name acted as an Open Sesame. She was given an appointment to view the collection that morning.

Two hours later she emerged dazed but triumphant. She could hardly believe she had just spent several thousand dollars on one black dress— but what a dress. It was breathtaking, from the shirred torso which made her waist seem minuscule to the silky handkerchief hemline drifting around her calves. The only uncertainty was the V of black lace outlined in diamonds which speared from between her breasts to her waist.

'Don't you think it's a little too revealing?' she'd asked Gada uneasily.

'It does not reveal. It hints,' he had told her severely. 'Trust me. You will be the envy of every woman at the awards, and not only because you wear a Gada original but because the formidable Reid Branden will be unable to take his eyes off you.'

Such a prospect had almost prompted her to reject the dress. It seemed too much like playing with fire. Then she became impatient with herself for letting Reid's opinion matter. The dress made her feel good and she was going to need every bit of confidence to face the glittering crowd at the banquet. If Reid couldn't control himself, she was hardly to blame.

Her doubts flooded back in earnest when he knocked on her door to announce it was time to leave. She had just finished arranging her hair into a knot at her nape, leaving a few strands curling around her face to soften the effect. Her ears needed some ornament, but all she possessed was costume jewellery which seemed an insult to the real diamonds encrusting the dress. She decided to leave her ears bare.

Her make-up was light, her one extravagance a ruby-red lipstick to lift the black of the dress. Her tongue tasted it nervously as Reid inspected her from head to toe. 'I trust you're satisfied with your investment,' she ventured as his assessment continued.

His finger traced the lace panel outlined in diamonds. The style forbade any thought of a bra and the cleft between her breasts was shadowed through the lace. It rose and fell as her breathing quickened.

'I'm more than satisfied,' he drawled. 'I may even forgo the awards altogether.'

So much for hinting. 'We...we can't,' she denied. 'You said yourself the company is a major sponsor.'

'Which surely gives me the right to choose whether I attend or not,' he observed, sending shivers of apprehension racing along her spine. She recognised now that she had chosen the dress as an act of defiance. How could she have been so foolhardy?

'I have an idea. Wait here,' he instructed.

Puzzled, she did as bidden, although strongly tempted to escape as far and as fast as possible. What did he have in mind? He was back before her racing mind had exhausted all the possibilities.

He held out a velvet-covered box. 'Put these on.'

Opening the box with shaking fingers, she beheld a pair of brilliant-cut diamond teardrop earrings set in gold. Her heart turned over. 'I can't, they're too much.'

'Even from a loving fiancé?'

From someone who fitted that description, they would be a personal gift to cherish. His words made a mockery of the very idea. 'No. I won't.'

'The earrings and the dress come together. Wear them both or wear nothing at all. It's your choice.'

'It would serve you right if I insisted on going to the banquet in my underwear,' she fumed at him.

His caressing gaze told her he was well aware of how little of the latter she was wearing. 'Now there's a tantalising thought, especially as you'd get no further than that doorway if you tried it.'

She hated to admit how much the idea inflamed her senses. Her fingers shook so badly that she dropped one earring as she tried to remove it from the box.

He scooped it up and palmed its mate. 'Allow me.'

Her bones turned liquid as he took her tender lobes between thumb and forefinger and fastened the diamond drops into place. As he removed his hand, he brushed her cheek and she had the strongest urge to turn her head until her lips grazed his palm. It was such an unexpected notion that tears sprang to her eyes.

She might have known he would notice them. 'Disappointed that we're going after all?' he queried provocatively.

His comment snapped her back to reality. 'Of course not. The sooner we get this over with, the better.'

He picked up her purse, another extravagance in the softest black kid to complement the dress, and handed it to her. 'I quite agree, but for different reasons.'

What they might be she could only guess at. By now she knew better than to ask.

Some of the biggest names in the international music industry were alighting from a cavalcade of limousines and making the trek up a red carpet to the hotel while the police restrained a tidal wave of eager fans.

Thankfully, Jo would have delivered Suzie backstage by now, ready for her starring role in tonight's ceremony, and away from this insanity. Penny wished someone could have spirited *her* out of it, but Reid had made it clear that Suzie needed her support. Not that *he* needed her, she noted. Still, she had little choice but to see it through.

Their limousine door was opened and she was helped out, closely followed by Reid, their arrival greeted by a barrage of exploding flashbulbs. She felt his arm tighten around her and leaned gratefully against him. 'You're doing fine,' he murmured against her ear.

His confidence inspired her and she managed to smile at the television cameras pointing their way. 'It's Reid Branden and his fiancée,' she heard over and over as they made their way inside.

She felt a thrill of pride as she looked up into Reid's handsome face at the behest of a photographer. Flash. His strong profile was imprinted on her mind. Why hadn't she noticed before how the suggestion of a dimple cratered his chin when he smiled? Or how austerely elegant his dark eyebrows were, framing those arresting, deep-set eyes?

Some time in the small hours of the morning they would retire to a suite on the higher floors of this hotel. The thought sent a thrill of quite unwarranted excitement pulsating through her.

The feeling so annoyed her that she hardly noticed they had completed their entrance and were now safely inside the banquet room.

Everybody wanted to talk to Reid but he kept her close by his side, shielded by his arm around her. For her part she knew very few people: a handful from the advertising world, Aloys Gada who beamed approval at her appearance in his gown, and a less approving Tonia Rigg.

'Amazing what they can do with copies these days,' she murmured when their paths crossed.

'It's a pleasure to see you, too, Tonia,' Penny said through a plastic smile. She was sure the other woman had seen Gada greeting her moments before so felt no need to defend herself. 'How have you been?'

Tonia swallowed some champagne. 'How should I be? I'm here with Jim Carrington of Carrington Records. He's desperate to have me as his PA.' She gave a brittle laugh. 'He's desperate to have me, period.'

Penny was relieved when Reid called her away to meet some more industry luminaries. Tonia's behaviour seemed uncharacteristically febrile. The champagne wasn't helping.

The awards were being televised so the presentations were timed around commercial breaks and the live musical performances by the young stars.

Suzie was among the last to perform, and by this time the noise, the glitter and the smoke had begun to take a toll. All the same, Penny felt a thrill of pride as Suzie moved into the spotlight, her white floor-length gown making her look utterly angelic.

In the hush before she began to play, her eyes sought Penny's as if for reasurance. Unobtrusively, Penny lifted her hand, the thumb and forefinger making an OK sign. Suzie's head came up as she recognised it, and she bent to the clarinet. The poignant Mozart piece filled the room.

Whatever this night had cost Penny, it was worth it, she resolved as she witnessed the mesmerising effect Suzie's playing exerted over the audience. Reid was right. She deserved this chance and all the others which would come after it.

Her young face was flushed as she lowered the instrument to deafening applause. With a graceful sweep of her skirts she acknowledged the audience like a professional then disappeared into the wings.

Penny half stirred and felt Reid's hand on her arm. 'Stay.'

And admit how tortured her emotions had become as a result of the haunting music? 'I came for Suzie,' she said raggedly. 'I should go back-stage and congratulate her.'

'There'll be time at the dinner afterwards,' he pointed out, his jaw set. 'It would be a pity for you to miss the rest of the programme.'

What else could possibly concern her? she wondered wildly. Her headache was getting worse and she had done her duty by being at his side thus far.

She hadn't disappointed Suzie, either, so why did he insist on her seeing this out to the bitter end?

She soon found out the reason.

Reid was called to the podium twice, once to present an award and again to receive an accolade for his own contributions to the music industry.

Was this what he had wanted her to see? To remind her yet again of all she had lost? It was effective, if so. Seeing him approach the podium, she felt a fierce sense of hunger, of possessiveness, which cut through the pain in her head and created a new one around her heart. Her breathing felt constricted and she knew it wasn't just the closeness of the room. Without being aware of it she had joined the rest of the audience on its feet, applauding as keenly as they. What was happening here?

The spotlight hit him, sculpting the ruggedly masculine planes of his face, and Penny's heart swelled, although she tried to contain the feeling. He looked so splendid in the golden light, his impossibly broad shoulders delineated by the fine cut of his dinner-jacket, his dress shirt in brilliant contrast, highlighting the healthy glow of his skin. When he approached the microphone a hush fell over the room and she found herself holding her breath.

His speech was simple but dignified as he thanked the industry members for the honour accorded him. Then the MC leaned across and whispered something. Reid shook his head. More prompting followed and a gorgeous young woman, obviously primed, walked on to the stage carrying a clarinet.

The applause rose to a crescendo as the audience recognised the MC's efforts to persuade Reid to play for them. Finally he held up his hands in acknowledgement and accepted the instrument.

There was a moment's delay while he tightened and checked it to his satisfaction then he stepped to the microphone. His eyes sought and held hers across the ballroom. 'I'd like to dedicate this composition to the beautiful lady who has agreed to become my wife. For all of you, but especially for Penelope—the Andretti Concerto.'

To more applause they resumed their seats and he began to play. The haunting notes built and built like the waves coming in from the ocean. She could almost hear night falling as the melody became darker, more brooding as the ocean played in the background.

Pain warred with pleasure inside her as the music spoke to her very soul. Tears gathered behind her closed lids. Of all the music he could have played, why did he have to choose the Andretti? Its bittersweetness pierced her to her core. Was *this* what he had wanted her to hear?

If only he hadn't played it in homage to a non-existent love match. At least non-existent as far as he was concerned. For her it emphasised the gulf which yawned between them.

By the time he returned to the table to the accompaniment of thunderous applause, her tension had resolved itself into a vicious migraine which made her feel impossibly fragile. Tears clouded her eyes as Reid brought her hand to his lips in a kiss of public homage she was sure was only for the benefit of those around them.

'I've never heard anything more beautiful,' she told him sincerely, as longings she dared not name engulfed her.

'I had planned a less public unveiling of it,' he told her wryly. 'You know why I played it, don't you?'

She knew what reason she wanted him to give but she was wishing for the moon. 'It sounded like the music of a man who's been away from Australia for too long,' she said, her voice unconsciously softening.

His assessing gaze lingered on her. 'Much too long.'

Then they were swept up in the remaining awards and finally the blazing television lights were turned off, the cameras trundled away, and everyone could relax. Jo and Suzie joined them for a while, Suzie overwhelmed by the congratulations she received from far and wide. Penny had a feeling it was something her niece would have to get used to.

By the time Jo decided that it was time to take Suzie home, Penny wished desperately that she could go with them. By now her headache was punishing. She yearned to slip away somewhere quiet, if only for a few minutes.

Her chance came when Reid was called away to another table. Excusing herself, Penny escaped to the ladies' room. She was splashing cold water on to her temples when a familiar voice accosted her.

'Well if it isn't Miss Accident-Prone Sullivan. I hope you aren't driving home tonight.'

It was a cruel reminder of the last time she and Tonia had left an industry function together. 'No, I'm not driving. Reid and I are staying here for the night.'

She had the satisfaction of seeing Tonia's face fall. She had obviously enjoyed the liberal amounts of vintage champagne on offer and her eyes were wild. 'You think you've won, don't you?'

'This isn't a contest, Tonia.'

'Isn't it? What about the saying about the spoils going to the victor—or don't you count those diamond trinkets as spoils?'

Unthinkingly Penny's hand went to her ear and touched the jewel Reid had fastened there. 'Reid wanted me to wear these.'

'I suppose he told you he bought them just for you?'

No explanation had been offered. 'Does it matter?'

'They were supposed to be *my* birthday present. Ask him if you don't believe me.'

Penny drew herself up, more shaken than she wanted Tonia to see. 'It hardly matters, since I'm the one wearing them, does it?' Leaving Tonia for once lost for words, she made as dignified an exit as she could.

She told herself it really didn't matter why Reid had bought the earrings, since she considered them on loan for the occasion. Their engagement wasn't genuine so she had no intentions of keeping such a valuable gift. All the same, Tonia's comment rankled, adding to the pain throbbing relentlessly through Penny's temples.

'You look pale. Would you like to leave?' Reid asked her when she returned to the table.

'But you're a guest of honour. I can't ask you to leave just because I have a headache.'

He rose and pulled out her chair. 'That settles it. We're going upstairs.'

Even so, it took ages to cross the room by the time Reid responded to the many well-wishers who intercepted them. By the time they reached the sanctuary of their suite Penny was almost drugged with pain.

Snapping on lights, he guided her to a sumptuous bedroom overlooking a jewelled vision of the city by night. Their luggage awaited on a stand nearby and she turned to it, blindly fumbling for a nightdress.

Abruptly the filmy garment was lifted from her fingers and strong hands went to the back fastening of her gown. 'You're almost out on your feet. Let me.'

Through the haze of pain, his touch was so gentle that she wanted to weep as he slid the zipper down and eased the dress over her hips so she could step clear of it. 'Gently,' he admonished when she swayed. The silken folds of her nightgown were eased over her head, then he slid an arm under her knees and placed her carefully on to the enormous bed.

He left her briefly, returning moments later with a glass of effervescent liquid. 'Soluble aspirin,' he explained as he held the glass to her lips.

Afterwards he made her lie face down while he massaged her shoulders and neck, the movements easing the tension knotting her muscles.

It felt so good that she wondered if she was dreaming. Surely Reid hadn't abandoned a glittering evening at which he was the undisputed star to minister to her? She was almost afraid to question his motives, although she was sure they had nothing to do with love. That was all on her side. Like it or not, Tonia's comments still rankled, if only as a reminder of how things really were between them.

'How's the headache now?' he asked as his strong musician's fingers continued the blissful kneading action at the top of her spine.

'Much better,' she murmured dreamily. It was hard to believe, but the blinding pain was almost gone. In its place was a delicious warmth which owed nothing to the aspirin, and everything to the sensuous touch of Reid's hands along her spine.

He had hands which could melt stone, she thought, so warm, so demanding. How many female bodies had he warmed with those irresistible hands? All the same she felt a shock like a betrayal when he stopped.

Rolling over, she looked to see where he had disappeared to, not wanting to admit to herself that she missed him already.

He came back carrying two glasses. 'Brandy,' he said softly. 'I thought it might help you to sleep.'

She sat up, resisting the impulse to gather the nightgown around herself, and took the glass. 'Thank you.'

The first sip of the brandy was like liquid fire as it slid down her throat. Or was it the primordial look he gave her over the rim of his own glass. Either way, an answering fire tore along her nerve-endings and exploded in flames somewhere near her heart. Their agreement was almost at an end. This was probably the last night they would spend together. She felt the flames threaten to consume her heart altogether.

When he lifted the glass from her unresisting fingers, his touch fanned the flames inside her until she could hardly breathe. She heard the tiny crystal sound as he set the glasses down, his own breathing sounding loud in the quiet room. Without a word he pulled her against him and she blessed the low level of lighting which concealed the bright flush she felt blooming on her skin. She loved this man, she accepted with a sense of wonder. Still loved him, for she had never really stopped. She saw it now with stunning clarity. In his arms she could no longer deny it, even as she accepted that this was all she would ever know of heaven.

Such a short time ago she would have celebrated her coming freedom. Now the thought of living without Reid plunged her into despair. He had offered her marriage and for an insane moment she considered accepting, if only to keep him by her side.

But without love it wouldn't work. Didn't she have her own parents' example of how a past mistake could eventually destroy a relationship? Knowing how she felt about Reid, she couldn't bear to take the risk.

There was still tonight, she reminded herself. The sweetness of Reid's embrace was almost unbearable for knowing it was the last time. She couldn't help opening her eyes to drink in the sight of him, his magnificently sculpted head so close to hers, his breath a soft wind on her face. Unconsciously, her half parted lips invited his kiss and her heart almost stopped as he granted her unspoken wish.

She was unable to restrain the tears which slid down her cheeks even as she abandoned herself to the ecstasy of being held in his arms.

He traced the droplets with his finger. 'Headache still bad? You should have told me.'

'No, it isn't the pain.' If you didn't count an agony of spirit which was almost beyond her capacity to endure. She forced her eyes away, making herself ask the question which rose unbidden into her mind. 'Tell me, when is Tonia Rigg's birthday?'

He frowned distractedly. 'About two days after she resigned. Why?'

So the earrings could well have been meant as a gift for her. Penny tried to tell herself she didn't care but with little success. 'Just something I heard at the dinner,' she said as lightly as she could. 'It's not important.'

He planted a butterfly kiss on the corner of her mouth. 'Just as well you realise it. I can assure you I'm not giving Tonia a moment's thought right now.'

If only she could be sure. She shifted slightly. 'I enjoyed your performance tonight.' Her voice thickened at the memory of his power to move her.

He chose to misunderstand and began to caress her in ever more mind-shattering ways. 'It's nothing compared to the encore,' he promised. It wasn't.

For a long time after Reid's even breathing told her he was asleep she lay awake, drinking in the sight of him at rest, his absurdly long lashes feathering his cheekbones, his sensuous mouth slightly parted.

A shadow darkened his lower lip where she'd nipped it in a frenzy of passion and she flushed guiltily. It was a sign he wasn't meant to read and she could only hope it would have faded by the morning.

Thankfully it was much less obvious by the time he'd shaved and breakfasted and they were ready to leave the hotel. His manner was so gentle, so considerate towards her that it was tempting to read more into it than she should.

'Do you have to work today?' she asked as they drove back to Kangaluma. His time with her was now so short that she wanted to guard every minute of it jealously. Why had she agreed to that foolish deadline?

'I'm afraid so,' he said almost regretfully. 'I have an important meeting this morning but I should be able to wrap it up by lunchtime. We'll go to Watson's Bay and have lunch on the beach at Doyle's.'

If he had suggested sitting outside and watching the grass grow she would have agreed if only for the chance to extend her time with him. But he'd probably chosen the famous seafood restaurant so they could be seen together. 'I'd like that,' she agreed, trying to push his motives out of her mind. 'It will be a kind of farewell lunch.'

He went quiet. 'How so?'

'In a week's time, this will all be behind us.' She kept her tone carefully light so he wouldn't see how much the admission cost her. 'Have you thought of how you're going to announce our supposed break-up?'

'You're really so anxious to have it over with?'

There was something so brittle in his voice that she wanted to cry. Not me, never me, she told herself. 'I thought it was what you wanted,' she supplied. 'It is what we agreed, isn't it?'

'Yes it is.'

Tell me it's no longer what you want, she cried inside. Tell me the deadline was a colossal mistake and we can work it out. But he remained silent the rest of the way home.

Her heart ached as she greeted the builder who had become almost a fixture around the house. 'Nearly finished, love,' he told her cheerfully, unaware that his words were hastening the breaking of her heart.

A letter lay on the hall table where the builder had collected it for her and she picked it up incuriously. It bore the crest of a well-known legal firm.

'Problems?' Reid queried when he heard her sharp intake of breath.

The eyes she turned to him were shining. 'You could say so. It's from Jo's husband, Andrew, through his lawyer. Jo must have told him about our engagement and now they say I no longer ''need'' the house under the terms of our inheritance. Can I be legally compelled to sell the house in order to give Jo her share, as these people claim?'

He took the letter from her trembling fingers and scanned it quickly, frowning. 'Such a loosely worded will as your father's was always open to challenge. A determined lawyer might well have a case.'

'But it's too soon. I haven't enough money to buy her out and I can't fight my own family in a court. I have to see Jo, get her to tell Andrew that he's wrong, we're not really engaged.' She clutched at his arm. 'You have to tell her the truth.'

He shook his head. 'It won't help because the truth is—I do want to marry you.'

CHAPTER TEN

HORROR transfixed her. Did he really want the house so much that he would let her be forced into selling? 'I don't believe you,' she flung at him, feeling as if someone was shaking her very foundations. 'If you won't do it, I'll tell Jo myself. It isn't as if she needs the money for herself.'

His iron grip on her wrist stayed her flight. 'I'm afraid she does.'

'What do you mean?'

'I didn't want to be the one to tell you, but you leave me no choice. Some of my business associates work with Jo's husband. It seems he made some bad business decisions lately and is on the verge of bankruptcy.'

'But the overseas trip...'

'No doubt Jo thought it was for pleasure. According to my sources, it was the easy way out for Kimber. It doesn't look as if he's coming back.'

She slumped into a chair and buried her face in her hands. She felt guilty for resenting Jo's happiness, although her own envy couldn't possibly have influenced the situation. 'I felt so badly because I thought she had everything—a loving husband, a beautiful child. I never dreamed...'

'No one did, least of all your sister. It makes Andrew's action easier to understand, doesn't it?'

Easier to understand but not necessarily easier to bear. Well, Reid had inadvertently done them a favour after all. By making the house more valuable he had ensured a larger share for Jo, because Penny intended to divide the proceeds equally. How could she do less when her sister was in such dire straits?

'I'm going to see her,' she resolved, standing up.

'Do you want me to come with you?'

Wanting desperately to say yes, she forced herself to give a shake of her head. Whatever comfort his presence afforded her would be paid for in loneliness once they separated for good. Now she wouldn't even have her home for consolation. Everything would be gone. 'You said your meeting is important,' she managed. 'This is a family affair.'

'Naturally.' His curt response drew her questioning glance but his face was a granite mask. 'If you're sure it's what you want?'

No, it isn't what I want, she wanted to scream. I want you to take me in your arms and tell me you love me, that everything's going to be all right. That my world isn't falling apart and I won't be left more alone than I've ever been before.

Accepting the futility of her thoughts, she forced a tremulous smile. 'I'm sure.' To her astonishment he dropped his hands to her shoulders and pulled her quickly against him, his lips moving against her hairline. His touch was fire but so fleeting that it took her senses a moment after he pulled away to register the effect. 'I'll see you at lunchtime,' was all he said before he strode away.

Jo's expression was guarded when Penny arrived at her door. 'I take it you've heard from Andrew's lawyer?'

Without waiting for an invitation Penny followed her inside, noting the disarray which was so uncharacteristic of her sister. A large box of tissues sat on a couch, several used ones wadded beside it. Tears were also out of character for Jo. 'I know why he's doing this,' she said without preamble.

Jo looked away. 'Then you know Andrew might not be coming back. His business is in a lot of trouble.'

Penny's heart went out to her sister, who had always seemed so assured, so confident. Now she was merely an older, equally vulnerable human being. 'Did you know when you came back to Australia?'

'I didn't want to accept it, but it was obvious when he wouldn't fly home after reading about Suzie. He didn't seem to care any more.' Her eyes brimmed and she twisted her hands together. 'Oh, Pen, what am I going to do? I still love him desperately yet he won't let me help him. Even telling him about you and Reid didn't give him hope.'

'The house will fetch a good price now it's all done up.' Penny had to resist the knife-like thrust which pierced her heart at the words. 'Your half-share will give you both enough money to start again.'

Jo's pathetically grateful look was almost reward enough to make the sacrifice worthwhile. 'You'd be so generous, even though my husband is the one forcing you to sell that old house you love so much?'

Penny stiffened her jaw. 'He isn't forcing me to do anything. I want to help.'

Suddenly they were in each other's arms. It was the first time Jo had hugged her since she was a little girl and it felt good, although Penny wished desperately that it had come about for happier reasons. 'I can't believe this is real,' Jo sniffed. 'I truly thought Andrew and I had the world at our feet.'

'Have you told Suzie yet?'

'I've been trying to work up the courage. She doesn't even know that Andrew might not be coming back.'

'I don't believe you. It's a rotten lie.'

The animal-like cry of pain from the doorway brought Penny's head around. The teenager had heard everything, she saw from the shock on Suzie's white face. 'It's your fault,' she threw at Jo. 'You drove him away. Well, I'm going, too. My family could be breaking up and you weren't going to tell me.'

'I was, honestly.' Jo's voice was a paralysed whisper. 'I love you.'

Suzie looked defiant but her lip trembled. 'Don't talk to me about honesty. You told me you loved my father but you're willing to give up on him. How can I believe you when you say you love me?'

Then she was gone and doors slammed throughout the house. 'You'd better go after her,' Penny urged. Jo needed no second bidding. Penny sat alone in the living-room, finding herself reaching for the box of tissues. What a mess it all was.

Jo was back minutes later, looking distressed. 'She's left the house, Pen. I can't find her anywhere. Where could she have gone?'

The telephone interrupted Penny's answer. White-faced, Jo took it. But it wasn't Suzie. 'It was Andrew, he's at the airport. Oh, Penny, he's coming home after all.' Jo's voice shook with emotion and her eyes brimmed. 'I have to find Suzie and tell her everything's going to be all right.'

Penny was almost in tears herself. 'I'm so happy for you, Jo. It *will* be all right. And we'll find Suzie, don't worry. You try ringing all her school friends. She may go to one of them.' Another inspiration struck. 'She could turn to Reid; he's been a good friend to her.'

'Shall I call him?'

'No, you start on her friends. I'll go to his office. If she's there we'll bring her straight back.'

Jo's look was heart-rending. 'Thank you, Pen. I couldn't bear it if anything happened to her just when everything looks promising again.'

'It isn't going to,' Penny admonished her, hoping it was true. Suddenly she needed Reid's strength, his calmness under pressure. She needed him. 'I'd better get going.'

He was in the executive flat and yes, there was a lady with him, she was informed by Reid's new assistant when Penny reached his office. Relief made her feel weak. Suzie had turned to him after all. Penny hurried to his private lift.

But it wasn't Suzie who opened the door to her. It was Tonia looking as stunning as ever in a black mini skirt, matching jacket and frilled low-cut blouse. At the sight of Penny's agitated expression, she raised a finely pencilled eyebrow. 'Don't look so surprised. I warned you I'd be back.'

So this was the important appointment Reid had wanted to keep. Despair radiated through Penny, the discovery hurting more than anything she had ever endured. After all they had been to each other—was it only in the early hours of this morning?—she could hardly believe Reid had turned to Tonia so quickly. It underscored Penny's awareness that she was a passing fancy, a means to an end, the end being Kangaluma.

It took willpower but she held Tonia's gaze. 'I need to see Reid. I was told he was here.'

'He's in the bedroom.' Her lazy drawl dripped suggestiveness. 'I doubt whether he's interested in seeing you right now.'

Probably not but it wasn't going to stop her from enlisting his help. Right now Suzie's wellbeing meant more to Penny than her own feelings. She would have plenty of time to deal with those later, in private.

'All the same I intend to see him,' she said with the steely determination of one who has nothing left to lose. 'All you need to decide is whether I go past you or over you.'

Visibly nonplussed, Tonia decided that discretion was a good idea and stepped aside, affording Penny entry to the flat. Tonia swung around and reached for a handbag dangling from the back of a chair. On the chair lay several file folders. 'Fortunately I was just leaving anyway.'

'Who is it, Tonia?'

Penny felt her heart stop as Reid stepped into the room. He wore the cream linen trousers in which he'd left her house this morning but his chest was bare and he had a white towel slung across one shoulder. 'Damned stuff won't come out,' he muttered, freezing as he caught sight of Penny. There was a quick flaring of something in his gaze then his look turned civilly cool. 'Hello, Penny—you're early.'

She tried to still the racing of her heart which insisted on responding to the sight of him, his trousers riding low on narrow hips, a dark V of chest hair disappearing below the loosened leather belt. Hastily she lifted her gaze. 'Obviously much too early. But don't let me intrude. I came to see if you'd heard from Suzie.'

Instantly he was on alert. 'What happened?'

'She heard Jo telling me about Andrew. He *is* coming back. He's on the way home from the airport right now, but Suzie didn't wait to hear that part. She ran out of the house in a terrible state.'

'She hasn't called here. Tonia only arrived a few minutes ago. You didn't see her, did you?'

A tiny flame flickered to life inside Penny but she hastily doused it. What did it matter when Tonia arrived? His state of undress made it obvious what would have happened next.

'No, I didn't see her,' the other woman offered.

'But you got the files you wanted?' She nodded. 'Good. I knew you'd be back for them so I brought them up here for safe keeping. Was there anything else?'

It was so clearly a dismissal that Penny felt an unaccustomed surge of compassion for Tonia. Was she wrong about the situation? It seemed she was. 'No, there's nothing else, so I'll be off. You might try lemon juice for that stain on your shirt.'

Shouldering her bag, she tucked the files under her arm. Her murmured farewell was barely audible before the door whispered shut behind her.

Penny crossed her arms over her chest. 'What was that about lemon juice for a stain?'

'Got some ink from the damned computer printer on my shirt,' he grimaced. 'I was up here changing it when Tonia arrived looking for her personal tax files.'

'I see.'

His hard gaze transfixed her. 'You didn't seem too pleased to find Tonia here.'

She took refuge in evasion. 'It's none of my business.'

His fingers slid under her chin and he lifted her face to his. 'So you don't give a damn what we were doing?'

Not now she knew what was going on. But the admission was far too revealing so she lowered long lashes, veiling the truth he was bound to read in her eyes. 'It hardly matters now, does it?'

'Are you sure, Penny?'

No, she wasn't sure about anything any more except that she loved this man more than life itself. It was crazy to even think this way, when nothing could ever come of it, but she couldn't seem to stop herself.

It was only by concentrating on the reason why she was here that she managed to stop herself from melting into his arms and making a complete fool of herself by confessing everything.

'Suzie,' she reminded him hoarsely. 'We have to find her. Jo's almost mad with worry.'

He seemed to shake himself mentally. 'Has Jo checked with Suzie's friends?'

'They were the first people we thought to contact, then I thought of you.' Her voice dropped to a betraying huskiness.

He snapped his fingers. 'Her school!'

She bit her lip. 'It's a pupil-free day. There are no classes so why would she go there?'

'She already has the temperament of a musician. Unless I miss my guess we'll find her at the school's music studio, playing her heart out.' He gave her a wry look. 'Music can be a handy outlet for one's emotions when things get too much.'

'Oh, lord, I hope you're right.'

'So do I.' Releasing her, he headed towards the bedroom. 'I'll get dressed and drive you there in my car; it's faster. In the meantime, call Jo and tell her to meet us there.'

She did as bidden, dialling Jo's number with shaking fingers. All the time she was achingly conscious of the sounds coming from the next room as Reid changed with the speed of light. Despite the crisis, her errant imagination insisted on supplying graphic images of him stripped to the waist, his magnificent torso gleaming in the morning light, every muscles delineated like a Rodin sculpture.

It was just as well her hands were occupied with the telephone or she might have given in to the almost overpowering impulse to join him in the next room.

It took several attempts before she was able to talk to Jo. The busy line told her Jo still hadn't located Suzie. 'No one's seen her all morning,' her sister told her in a tremulous voice.

Penny relayed Reid's message, ending with his assurance that Suzy would be where he predicted. 'I'm sure it will be all right,' she said as she hung up.

At least one good thing had to come out of this whole débâcle.

CHAPTER ELEVEN

REID emerged wearing a navy blue tracksuit over a white polo-necked sweater. He looked stunningly athletic and breathtakingly handsome. She swallowed hard. 'Ready to go?'

'When you are. I'll notify my office on the way out in case she decides to drop in here after all.'

They had covered all the bases yet she still felt uneasy as they collected his car from the underground car park. It was the strain of being with him, feeling the way she did and being unable to express it, she told herself as he eased the powerful Mercedes out into the traffic. As he reached for the gearstick, his hand brushed her leg and she drew back in alarm at the rush of sensation the light touch provoked.

Her reaction drew a frown of annoyance, she saw when he glanced at her. He couldn't know that it wasn't rejection which made her draw back, but the fear that, if she let herself, she would give in to the almost unbearable impulse to return his touch with caresses of her own which would betray her state of mind utterly.

She kept a tense silence all the way along Falcon Street and Military Road, her arms drawn across herself in silent self-protection. Her relief was almost palpable as they approached the intersection where Suzie's school was located.

The school itself was set in parklike grounds but shared a boundary with a traffic-laden road. With difficulty Reid found a parking space along a quiet side street and they walked back to the main road. Reid's hand had come automatically under her arm and she felt his touch like a brand, burning through the filmy fabric of her blouse.

'There she is.' His triumphant observation startled her out of her reverie. Suzie was approaching the school, her square clarinet case swinging from her hand. Her young face was a study in unhappiness.

'Suzie,' Penny called gently, afraid of alarming the youngster but wanting to stop her before she disappeared among the labyrinthine school buildings.

The teenager's head came up. When she spotted Penny, she tossed her head in rejection. 'Go away. I don't want to talk to you.'

They were close enough to see the tears streaking her face. 'I know it hurts, darling, but we only want to help you,' Penny tried again.

'Sure you do, by providing the money to split up my family.'

Shocked, Penny stumbled to a halt, horrified by how her niece perceived the situation. 'It isn't like that,' she denied.

'Your father's on his way home right now,' Reid said in a gentle voice. 'He'll want you there to welcome him.'

'You're only saying that to make me feel better,' Suzie said, her voice thready with tears. She turned towards the pedestrian crossing outside the school.

'I heard what Mum said and I only want to be left alone.'

Without looking she stepped off the kerb. Head down, she moved on to the crossing at the same moment as a truck hurtled around the corner. After that everything seemed to happen in slow motion.

'Suzie, look out.' Penny knew her scream was too late and stood frozen to the spot in horror. How could anyone prevent what was about to happen?

It was the nightmare of the accident all over again and this time it was happening in broad daylight. The truck's horn blasted as the driver spotted the youngster in his path but the scream of brakes came too late to slow the behemoth's onrush.

Suddenly Reid was moving with a speed she wouldn't have believed humanly possible if she hadn't witnessed it. In a streak of motion he reached Suzie and thrust her out of the way with a powerful sweep of his arm. She went sprawling on to the footpath. Seconds later the truck barrelled across the spot where she'd been standing.

'Reid!' Penny's lungs almost burst with the scream which tore from her throat as the truck clipped him and sent him reeling against a tree beside the road. She felt the impact in her own body as he went down and the sight of him blurred in the tears fogging her vision.

'Please be all right,' she prayed as she hurried to his side. Suzie was on her feet, gathering up her belongings. She looked scared but unhurt.

Reid was another matter. There was something wrong, Penny saw as he got groggily to his feet, but he managed a shaky grin. 'Don't look so ter-rified. I'm fine. Just a little shaken up, that's all.'

'Are you sure? I couldn't stand it if you were hurt because I'd been a stupid jerk,' Suzie contrib-uted. 'I'm so sorry.'

His left arm stayed at his side as he used his right to ruffle the teenager's hair. 'Don't blame yourself. Your mother's just arrived and she has someone with her that I think you'll be pleased to see.'

A lump rose in Penny's throat as she caught sight of Jo and Andrew in each other's arms. Suzie let out a squeal of pure joy and ran to them. They were talking to the truck driver who'd left his cab to make sure everyone was all right. He had to stand aside as Suzie barrelled into her parents' arms. Penny's cheeks were damp.

Reid waved away Jo and Andrew's effusive thanks, urging them instead to take their daughter home and enjoy their reunion. The truck driver was also relieved to be on his way with no further re-criminations. He should have taken more care when approaching a pedestrian crossing, but no purpose would be served by making an issue of it now.

Finally Penny had her wish to be alone with Reid. Panic gripped her anew as he slumped against the tree. 'You are hurt.'

He passed his right hand over his eyes. 'I didn't want to scare Suzie but the fool truck caught me in the shoulder. Hurts like the devil but I don't think anything's broken.'

'All the same, you should see a doctor.'

He opened his eyes and amazingly, amusement warred with the pain reflected there. 'Don't tell me that's concern for my wellbeing I hear in your voice.'

Tears threaded her response. 'What did you expect? That I wouldn't care?'

'Do you?'

She was afraid to look at him lest he read the answer in her eyes. At that moment she felt nakedly transparent and it took all her willpower to answer lightly, 'Of course I do, as I would about anyone who's hurt.'

His right hand gripped her shoulder so tightly she would have bruises there tomorrow. She couldn't make herself care. 'Only that?'

'What else could there be?'

'I'm waiting to hear it from you.'

She shook her head. The memory of the truck was too fresh in her mind, too redolent of her dream about the accident. Dreams could turn to nightmares, as her parents' marriage testified. 'I can't.'

He seemed suddenly infinitely weary. 'Then let's get out of here. You'll have to drive. I don't think I can.'

He shrugged off the supportive arm she tried to offer him. Although he seemed steady enough on his feet, she noticed he made little use of his left arm. What if the injury was more serious than he thought and it affected his playing? She could hardly bear to consider a world without his music in it. Without *him* in it, the thought came and she caught her breath on a silent sob.

He handed her the car keys and she unlocked both doors then held the passenger door for him as he slid in. He fastened his seat belt one-handed, his expression grim. His breath whistled through his teeth as he brought the strap across his damaged shoulder. His face was ashen.

Her own body felt bruised and battered as if she and not he had been thrown across the road. Was this what it would always be like? Knowing he was there somewhere, sharing his pain but being unable to share anything else in his life?

'Damn!' The unaccustomed expletive flew from her lips as she got into the driver's side of the big Mercedes. 'I can't do this.'

'What is it? Shock setting in?'

She turned brimming eyes to him, her frustration mirrored there. 'I mean I don't know how to drive your car. I never learned to drive a manually geared car. My licence is only for an automatic.'

'*What did you say*?'

Feeling useless, she repeated, 'I can't drive your car. I'm sorry, but we'll have to get a taxi back.'

He caught the hand pounding the wheel in frustration. To her astonishment he brought it to his lips. 'My darling Penny, I've never been so pleased about anything in my life.'

He was pleased because she couldn't drive his car? The pain must be making him delirious. But his eyes were clear and his voice vibrant as he showed her how to use the car phone to summon a taxi.

The air of suppressed excitement was still there after they were dropped at Kangaluma, again at his insistence. 'Shouldn't we go straight to the hospital?' she asked anxiously.

'The hospital can wait. I have more pressing concerns,' he insisted, although the greyness of his features told her how hard he was battling to resist the pain of his injury. What was so urgent it was worth prolonging his suffering for?

He accepted a glass of whisky at least, swallowing it neat. It seemed to help a little.

'Now would you tell me why we had to come back here?' she asked. Couldn't he see what this was doing to her?

'You still don't get it, do you? All this time you were afraid I'd hold the accident against you in the future because of the way I feel about drunk drivers. Well, it isn't going to happen.'

'Of course it isn't.' Because there was no future for them.

'There's nothing which could possibly come between use, now or ever,' he went on as if she hadn't interrupted. 'You see, you couldn't have been driving that night.'

Her throat felt so raw it was an effort to force the words out. 'What are you talking about?'

He winced as he eased his damaged shoulder. 'The car you and Tonia were driving was manually geared. Now do you understand?'

A tightness banded her chest until she could hardly breathe. 'Oh, Reid! Then that means...'

'Tonia drove my cars regularly and they're all manually geared. So she must have placed you in the driver's seat after the accident, while you were knocked out.'

Penny pressed her fingers to her temples. 'I remember a little now. I didn't want either of us to drive so she said she'd fetch a driver. I waited in the passenger seat but she got in and activated the central locking system. I couldn't stop her and I couldn't get out. She said she'd be fine.'

He brushed a hand across her forehead. 'Sssh. It's all right. She fooled us both. I really thought she was unconscious when I found her, so I know what a good actress she can be. But it does explain your strong feeling that you weren't driving that night. You couldn't remember consciously, but your unconscious knew the truth.'

Crazily, Penny understood why Tonia had done it. The other woman loved Reid. Knowing how he felt about drink drivers, she couldn't risk losing his affection so she had allowed Penny to bear the brunt of his wrath. Ironically, she had lost the one thing she had risked everything to retain.

'Can you forgive me for doubting you?' His ragged appeal shook her to her core.

'Forgiveness implies a debt which simply doesn't exist,' she denied shakily. 'Who was it said love is never having to say you're sorry?'

His breath came in a shuddering sigh. 'In that case I may never apologise to you for anything as long as we live.'

Her courage almost deserted her, her bones turning liquid as she absorbed the import of his words. What if he didn't mean it the way it sounded? She decided she couldn't take the risk of any more misunderstandings. Nevertheless the words required a huge effort of will to force out. 'I shan't expect any apologies, because I love you.'

His right arm came around her and he pulled her against his good side to bestow a lingering kiss on her parted lips. Fire coursed through her veins. 'I never thought I'd hear you say it,' he admitted against her trembling mouth.

'I never thought I would, either. I thought you never wanted to see me again after the accident. The look on your face that night made your feelings so clear.'

'Not clear enough, evidently. My disgust was aimed at myself for allowing you to travel back to the hotel alone. I kept telling myself that if only I'd been there, I could have saved you that ordeal. It was myself I berated, not you, but you'd left the country before I could let you know.'

She turned molten eyes to him. 'When we were together you recoiled from my touch. And the film of your parents' accident was a further condemnation.'

His body turned rigid and his eyes narrowed until he opened them to caress her with a look. 'I recoiled because every time I touched you I was reminded of what I'd lost. As for the film, I destroyed it when I realised how much pain it caused you.'

The thought that he had begun to care even before he knew the truth about the accident made her heart swell so joyfully that she wanted to explode. 'When did you decide you loved me?' she asked shyly. 'There seemed so many things against us.'

His finger traced the outline of her full lips before she captured the tip, kissing it gently. 'Not as many as you might think. When I saw you at Kangaluma

I tried to convince myself it was the house I really wanted. But when we made love I realised I was kidding myself. It was the beautiful owner I loved. Working on the house was the best way I knew to get through to you.' He smiled lazily. 'It worked, didn't it?'

'You didn't give me much alternative,' she agreed. 'But whenever I dared think of a shared future, I was terrified that the past would come between us, as it did for my parents.'

'Nothing is going to come between us,' he stated so confidently that her heart leapt. 'I was already convinced of it when I bought you those earrings.'

'You bought them for me?'

'Did you doubt it?'

'Tonia told me they were for her birthday,' she confessed, ashamed to admit she had ever entertained any doubts, although they were born of her own insecurity rather than lack of faith in him.

'Tonia has a great deal to answer for,' he said grimly, his dark eyes clouding. 'When my lawyers have finished with her...'

She rested a hand on his good arm. 'Please, let it lie. I couldn't bear to have it all raked over again. It's enough for me to have you know the truth.'

He lifted her hand to his mouth kissing each finger in turn, sending shivers down her spine. 'You're more forgiving than me, but I'll do whatever makes you happy.'

'What would make me happy,' she said on a rising note of concern, 'would be for you to see a doctor about that shoulder.' He must be in agony but there was no way he was going to admit it.

His lips roved over her face and throat, setting her pulses racing. 'Is that the only way I can make you happy?'

'You know it isn't,' she denied, her voice trembling. 'But there'll be time enough for that later, once I know you're all right.'

He gave an exaggerated sigh. 'You're a hard woman, Penny Sullivan. And you make me a hard man, but I can see it won't do me any good until we get this little problem out of the way.'

She was suddenly shy of admitting that she wanted him as much as he wanted her. 'Do you think it will take very long?'

He bestowed a lingering kiss on her half-parted lips, the warmth in his touch enough to set her senses singing. 'I'll make damned sure it doesn't. It feels like a dislocation, so as soon as it's set I'll be as good as new.

'There's one more thing,' he said, staying her hand as she reached for the telephone to summon a taxi. 'Something I want to give you.'

In his love he had already given her the greatest gift in the universe. 'There's nothing more I want in all the world,' she breathed, sinking back into the heaven of his embrace. In spite of Reid's pain, she had a feeling they weren't going anywhere until he finished what he wanted to say.

'What about Kangaluma?'

'It doesn't matter. Home is anywhere I'm with you,' she said and meant it with all her heart. Much as she loved the old house, it meant nothing unless she could share it with Reid.

Which was exactly what he had in mind. 'I telephoned Andrew's lawyer this morning and made a cash offer in settlement of Jo's claim on the house. Her family gets immediate use of the money and Kangaluma stays in the family. Our family,' he added significantly.

She had a sudden breathtaking vision of children running helter-skelter through the house, their small beds filling the warren of rooms upstairs. 'There are a lot of rooms,' she said breathlessly.

'I think we can manage a child for each one.' His mellow tone made her tremble with the promise inherent in the statement.

'It should be fun trying,' she agreed.

His hand splayed across her back as he pressed her to him, his touch fiery through her clothing. His need for her drove her almost insane with longings of her own. He gave a ragged sigh. 'We'd better get to that doctor before I forget that I need one. The way you make me feel right now, it's a real possibility.'

'For me, too.' Her whispered confession invited a fresh assault on her mouth. 'I must remember to thank Suzie for bringing us together. Imagine, we might never have learned the truth about the accident, or found each other again, if she hadn't written you that letter.'

He *was* imagining it, and he went cold in spite of the burning agony in his shoulder. 'But she did,' he said hoarsely. 'She even tipped me off by adding that PS about the Andretti Concerto. Now I'm adding a PS of my own, as in, Penny Sullivan, I love you.'

He felt a thrill ripple through her and tightened his hold. 'It won't be PS for long. I'll be PB after we're married,' she commented.

'Don't be technical when I'm trying to be poetic,' he reproved. What she really needed was for him to wrap both arms around her so tightly she became dizzy. Except that one arm wasn't co-operating too well. Of all the times to get injured. On the other hand it could have been Suzie, he added to himself. It had been worth his suffering to see her get up and walk back to her parents.

And the woman in his arms—arm, he corrected himself—was worth waiting for. He'd soon be back in one piece, then he'd love her as she deserved to be loved. In the meantime he'd have to woo her with words. 'I love you, Penny Sullivan.'

She kissed him back with all the pent-up passion at her command. 'You don't know how wonderful it is to hear you say it.'

Maybe words had their uses after all. 'Then I'll say it again. I love you, love you, love you. Confound this arm.'

* * *

My darling Reid,

It's very late. The hospital is quiet and your one-day-old son is sleeping peacefully beside me so I'm writing to tell you how I feel about a few things.

Firstly, I'm as much in love with my talented husband as I was when we married. I'm thankful you were here for Francis's arrival although I'll miss being there when you collect your Oscar for best musical score, featuring the Andretti Concerto. When you first composed it for me in Sydney I knew it was special. I never dreamed it would inspire a film but I shan't mind sharing it with the world. In my heart it will always be 'our' music.

I'm glad you wanted to call the baby Francis after your father. I did wonder if your musical instincts would lean towards Amadeus or Ludwig. Suzie visited us after you left and swears that your son's chubby lips have the perfect *emboucher* to make a clarinet player. She'll be a wonderful godmother to him and when he's old enough I'll tell him how her letter to you brought us together.

Even with you flying straight back from Los Angeles, it will be another day before we're together. I can hardly wait. I miss you all so much: Emma and Jessie, our 'terrible twins' Brad and Josh, and little Gillian. Our family. You always said we'd fill the rooms at Kangaluma and we have. Just as you filled the empty spaces in my heart. Come home safely, my darling. I love you.

Your wife of eight magical years,
Penny

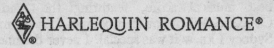

**Announcing
the New Pages & Privileges™ Program
from Harlequin® and Silhouette®**

Get All This FREE
With Just One Proof-of-Purchase!

- **FREE Travel Service** with the guaranteed lowest available airfares plus 5% cash back on every ticket

- **FREE Hotel Discounts** of up to 60% off at leading hotels in the U.S., Canada and Europe

- **FREE Petite Parfumerie** collection (a $50 Retail value)

- **FREE $25 Travel Voucher** to use on any ticket on any airline booked through our Travel Service

- **FREE Insider Tips Letter** full of fascinating information and hot sneak previews of upcoming books

- **FREE Mystery Gift** (if you enroll before June 15/95)

And there are more great gifts and benefits to come!
Enroll today and become Privileged!

(see insert for details)

 PROOF-OF-PURCHASE

Offer expires October 31, 1996   HR-PP2